"He walked to the fire and threw it in, remarking, 'Eternally —— my soul! (his favorite oath,) gentlemen, if I don't think we have lived long enough!' "—*Page* 105.

A QUARTER RACE IN KENTUCKY,

AND OTHER TALES.

"A rough-hewn fellow, who either was, or pretended to be, drunk, was bantering to run his mare against any horse that had ploughed as much that season."—*Page* 14.

EDITED BY W. T. PORTER, ESQ., OF THE N. Y. SPIRIT OF THE TIMES.

PHILADELPHIA:

T. B. PETERSON & BROTHERS.

A
QUARTER RACE IN KENTUCKY,

AND

OTHER SKETCHES,

ILLUSTRATIVE OF

SCENES, CHARACTERS, AND INCIDENTS,

THROUGHOUT

"THE UNIVERSAL YANKEE NATION."

EDITED BY

WILLIAM T. PORTER,

EDITOR OF "THE SPIRIT OF THE TIMES," "BIG BEAR OF ARKANSAS, AND OTHER TALES," ETC.

WITH ILLUSTRATIONS BY DARLEY.

Philadelphia:
T. B. PETERSON AND BROTHERS,
306 CHESTNUT STREET.

COLLINS, PRINTER.

INTRODUCTION.

THE great degree of favour with which a series of Sketches, similar to those embraced in the present volume, was received by the public and the press last year, has induced the publishers to add another volume of the same character and style to their "LIBRARY OF AMERICAN HUMOROUS WRITERS."

As "*The Big Bear of Arkansas*, and Other Tales," which were more especially intended to illustrate character and incident in the south and south-west, appear to have been unusually popular, the Editor trusts that the present volume, which includes a wider range of the peculiarities and characteristics of "the Universal Yankee Nation," will not be deemed less entertaining by the public generally.

The different Sketches in this volume have nearly all appeared in the columns of the New York "Spirit of the Times," where most of them were published originally. If they afford as much satisfaction in their present shape as when first given to the world, the Editor will enjoy the consciousness of having been the means of alleviating the dulness and *ennui* of many a weary hour, and of having added his mite in contributing to the amusement and gratification of "the million."

WM. T. PORTER.

Office of the "Spirit of the Times,"
New York, Oct. 1846.

CONTENTS.

A QUARTER RACE IN KENTUCKY.

BY A NORTH ALABAMIAN.

The following inimitable story, perhaps the most humorous of its kind in the language, was originally published in the N. Y. "Spirit of the Times," in 1836; since that period the unceasing demand for copies of it has rendered its re-publication necessary several times. It was written by a country gentleman of North Alabama, the author of "Jones's Fight." It is a matter of infinite regret that he cannot be induced to write more frequently; his friends would be "after him with a sharp stick," were we to disclose his name, which is familiar to tens of thousands of his countrymen, if they only knew it.

NOTHING would start against the Old Mare; and after more formal preparation in making weight and posting judges than is customary when there is a contest, "*the sateful old kritter*" went off crippling as if she was not fit to run for sour cider, and any thing could take the shine out of her that had the audacity to try it. The muster at the stand was slim, it having been understood up town, that as to sport to-day the races would prove a *water-haul*. I missed all that class of old and young gentlemen who annoy owners, trainers, and riders, particularly if they observe they are much engaged, with questions that should not be asked, and either can't or should not be answered. The business folks and men of gumption were generally on the *grit*, and much of the chaff certainly had been blown off.

A walk or gallop over is a slow affair; and without

being in any way able to account for it, it seemed to be an extremely dry affair; for while the four mile was *being* done (*as the prigs have it*) I noticed many a centaur of a fellow force his skeary nag up to the opening in the little clapboard shanty, and shout out impatiently—"Colonel, let us have some of your *byled* corn—pour me out a buck load—there—never mind about the water, I drank a heap of it yesterday," and then wheel off to the crowd as if intent on something.

The race, like all things, had an end, and I had some idea, in imitation of Sardanapalus, "all in one day to see the race, then go home, eat, drink, and be merry, for all the rest was not worth a fillip," when I met Dan. He knows a little, finds out a little, and guesses the rest, and, of course, is prime authority. I inquired if the hunt was up. "Oh, no, just hold on a while, and there will be as bursting a quarter race as ever was read of, and I will give it 'em, so you can make expenses." I always make a hand when about, and thinking I might get a wrinkle by prying into the mystery of quarter-racing, I accordingly rode to the thickest of the crowd. A rough-hewn fellow, who either was, or pretended to be, drunk, was bantering to run his mare against any horse that had ploughed as much that season, his mare having, as he assured us, tended twenty-five acres in corn. Another chap sidled up to him, and offered to plough against him for as much liquor as the company could drink, or for who should have both nags—his horse had never run, as he did not follow it. Sorrel got mad, and offered to beat him in the cart, wagon or plough, or he could beat him running one hundred miles, his weight on each, for five hundred dollars. Bay still disclaimed racing, but would run the quarter stretch, to amuse the company, for one hundred dollars. Sorrel took him up, provided Bay carried his present rider, and he would get somebody; Bay agreed, provided he would not get a lighter rider. It was closed at that, and two of Senator Benton's abominations—$100 United States Bank Bills—were planked up. Bay inquired if they could stand another $50;—agreed to by Sorrel, who, observing Bay shell out a $100 note, said, there was no use of making change, as his note was the same amount, and they might as well go the $100. This was promptly agreed to, and another one hundred dollars offered, and immediately covered—there being now three hundred dollars aside. Now came a proposal to increase it three hundred dollars more; Bay said—"You oversize my pile, but if I can borrow the money, I'll accommodate you," and immediately slipped off to consult his banker. Dan now whispered, "*Spread yourself on the Bay.*" Thinking I should run in while I was hot, I observed aloud—I should admire to bet some gentleman ten dollars on the bay. A Mr. Wash, or as he was familiarly called, Big Wash, snapped me up like a duck does a June-bug, by taking the bill out of my hand, and observing that either of us could hold the stakes, put it in his pocket. Finding this so easily done, I pushed off to consult my friend Crump, the most knowing man about short races I ever knew, and one who can see as far into a millstone as the man that pecks it. I met him with the man that made the race on the bay, coming to get a peep at the sorrel. As soon as he laid eyes on her he exclaimed—

"Why, Dave, you made a pretty pick up of it; I'm afraid our *cake is all dough*—that's old Grapevine, and I told you point blank to walk round her, but you're like a member of the Kentucky legislature, who admitted that if he had a failing it was being a *leetle* too brave."

"How could I know Grapevine," replied Dave, doggedly; "and you told me you could beat her, any how."

"Yes," said Crump, "I think I can; but I didn't come a hundred and fifty miles to run them kind of races—Old Tompkins has brought her here, and I like him for a *sucker!*"

"Well," says Dave, "maybe I can get off with the race if you think you'll be licked."

"No," said Crump, "when I go a catting, I go a catting; its mighty mixed up, and there's no telling who's constable until the election is over; it will be like the old bitch and the rabbit, nip and tack every jump, and sometimes the bitch a *leetle* ahead."

Old Tompkins, who had not appeared during the making of the race, now came round, and seeing the bay, said—"Popcorn, by G—d." He now came forward, and addressed the other party: "Boys," said he, "it's no use to run the thing into the ground. If a man goes in for betting, I say let him go his load, but we have no ambition against you, so draw the bet to one hundred dollars; that is enough for a little tacky race like this, just made for amusement."—Carried by acclamation.

Now the judges were selected: a *good* judge does not mean exactly the same thing here as on the bench, though some of the same kind may be found there—it means one who is obstinate in going for his own friends. It did not seem to be considered courteous to object to the selections on either side, perhaps from a mutual consciousness of invulnerability. But one of the nominees for the ermine was a hickory over any body's persimmon in the way of ugliness. He was said to be the undisputed possessor of the celebrated jack-knife ; his likeness had been moulded on dog-irons to frighten the children from going too near the fire, and his face ached perpetually ; but his eyes! his eyes! He was said to have caught a turkey-buzzard by the neck, the bird being deceived, and thinking he was looking another way ; and several of the crowd said he was so cross-eyed he could *look at his own head!* It was objected to him that he could not keep his eyes on the score, as he did not see *straight*, and it was leaving the race to the accident of which of his optics obtained the true bearing when the horses were coming out. The objections were finally overruled, the crooked party contending that Nature had designed him for a quarter judge, as he could station one eye to watch when the foremost horse's toe struck the score, and could note the track of the horse that followed, at the same moment, with the other eye.

The riders now attracted my attention. It is customary, I believe, to call such "a feather," but they seemed to me about the size of a big Christmas turkey gobbler, without feathers ; and I was highly delighted with the precocity of the youths—they could swear with as much energy as men of six feet, and they used fourth-proof oaths with a volubility that would bother a congressional reporter.

There now arose a dispute as to whether they should run to or from the stand, it being a part of the mile track, and there being some supposed advantage to one of the horses, or the other, according as this might be arranged. It was determined by a toss-up at last, to run to the stand. After another toss for choice of tracks, and another for the word, the horses walked off towards the head of the stretch. Now it was "Hurra, my Popcorn—I believe in you—come it strong, lumber—go it with a looseness—root little pig, or die." And, "Oh! my Grapevine! tear the hind sights off him!—you'll lay him out cold as a wagon-tire—roll your bones—go it, you cripples!" &c., &c., &c.

Beginning to doubt, from all I heard, whether my friend Dave had been regularly appointed almanac-maker for this year, I hedged a five, and staked it with a young man that was next me, riding a remarkable wall-eyed horse, and some time after staked another five dollars, with a person I had noticed assisting about the bar, and would be able to recognise again. I now flattered myself on my situation—I had all the pleasurable excitement of wagering, and nothing at risk.

Each side of the track was lined with eager faces, necks elongated, and chins projected, a posture very conducive to health in a bilious climate, as it facilitates the operation of emetics. I was deafened with loud cries of "Clear the track!" "Stand back!" "Get off the fence!" "The riders are mounted!" "They are coming!" "Now they are off!"—but still they came not. Without intending it, I found myself, and indeed most of the crowd, moving up towards the start, and after every failure, or false alarm, I would move a few yards. I overheard a fellow telling with great glee—"Well, I guess I warmed the wax in the ears of that fellow with the narrow brimmed white hat; he had an elegant watch that he offered to bet against a good riding-horse. You know my seventeen year old horse, that I always call the bay colt; I proposed to stake him against the watch, and the fellow agreed to it without ever looking in his mouth; if he had, he would have seen teeth as long as tenpenny nails. It is easy fooling any of them New York collectors—they ain't cute: the watch is a bang-up lever, and he says if he was GOING TO TRAVEL he would not be without it for any consideration. He made me promise if I won it to let him have it back at one hundred dollars in case he went into Georgia this fall. It is staked in the hands of the Squire there;—Squire, show it to this here entire stranger." The Squire produced a splendid specimen of the tin manufacture; I pronounced it valuable, but thought it most prudent not to mention for what purpose.

Alarms that the horses were coming continued, and I gradually reached the starting place: I then found that Crump, who was to turn Popcorn, had won the word—that is, he was to ask "are you ready?" and if answered "yes!" it was to be a race. Popcorn jumped about like a pea on a griddle, and fretted greatly—he was all over in a lather of sweat. He was managed very judiciously, and every attempt was made to soothe him and keep him cool, though he evidently was somewhat exhausted. All this time Grapevine was led about as cool as a cucumber, an awkward-looking *striker* of old Thompson's holding her by the cheek of the bridle, with instructions, I presume, *not to let loose in any case*, as he managed adroitly to be turning round whenever Popcorn put the question.

Old Tompkins had been sitting doubled up sideways, on his sleepy-looking old horse—it now being near dark—rode slowly off a short distance, and hitched his horse: he deliberately took off his coat, folded it carefully, and laid it on a stump; his neckcloth was with equal care deposited on it, and then his weather-beaten hat; he stroked down the few remaining hairs on his caput, and came and took the mare from his striker. Crump was anxious for a start, as his horse was worsted by delay; and as soon as he saw Grapevine in motion to please her turner, Old Tompkins swung her off ahead, shouting triumphantly, "Go! d—n you!" and away she went with an *ungovernable*. Crump wheeled his horse round before reaching the poles, and opened on Old Tompkins—"That's no way; if you mean to run, let us run, and quit fooling; you should say 'Yes!' if you mean it to be a race, and then I would have turned loose, had my nag been tail forward; it was no use for me to let go, as it would have been no race any how until you give the word."

Old Tomkins looked as if the boat had left him, or like the fellow that was fighting, and discovered that he had been biting his own thumb. He paused a moment, and without trying to raise a squabble, (an unusual thing,) he broke down the track to his mare, slacked her girths, and led her back, soothing and trying to quiet her. She was somewhat blown by the run, as the little imp on her was not strong enough to take her up soon. They were now so good and so good, and he proposed they should lead up and take a fair start. "Oh!" said Crump, "I thought that would bring you to your milk, so lead up." By this time you could see a horse twenty yards off, but you could not be positive as to his colour. It was proposed to call in candles. The horses were led up, and got off the first trial. "Ready?" "Yes!"—and a fairer start was never made. Away they went in a hurry,

"Glimmering through the gloam."

All hands made for the winning post. Here I heard —"Mare's race!"—"No! she crossed over the horse's path!"—"The boy with the shirt rode foul!"—"The horse was ahead when he passed me!" After much squabbling, it was admitted by both parties that the nag that came out on the left-hand side of the track was ahead; but they were about equally divided as to whether the horse or the mare came through on the left-hand side. The judges of the start agreed to give it in as even. When they came down, it appeared that one of the outcome judges got angry, and had gone home an hour ago. My friend that looked so many ways for Sunday, after a very ominous silence, and waiting until frequently appealed to, gave the race to the horse by ten inches. This brought a yell from the crowd, winners and losers, that beat any thing yet; a dozen of men were produced, who were ready to swear that gimblet-eye was a hundred yards off, drinking a stiff cock-tail at the booth, and that he was at the far side of it when the horses came out, and consequently must have judged the result through two pine planks an inch thick; others swore he did not know when the race was won, and was not at the post for five minutes after. Babel was a quiet retired place compared with the little assemblage at this time: some bets were given up, occasional symptoms of a fight appeared, a general examination was going on to be assured the knife was in the pocket, and those hard to open were opened and slipped up the sleeve; the crowd clustered together like a bee-swarm. This continued until about nine o'clock, when Crump, finding he could not get the stakes, compromised the matter, and announced that by agreement it was a drawn race.

B

This was received with a yell louder, if possible, than any former one; every one seemed glad of it, and there was a unanimous adjournment to the bar. Though tired and weary, I confess that I (for no earthly reason that I can give but the force of example) was inclined to join them, when I was accosted by a person with whom I had bet, and had staked in the hands of the young man riding the wall-eyed horse. "Well," said he, "shell out my five dollars that I put up with that friend of yours—as I can't find *him*." I protested that I did not know the young man at all, and stated that he had my stake also. He replied that I need not try to feed him on *soft corn* that way, and called on several persons to prove that I selected the stakeholder, and we were seen together, and we must be acquainted, as we were both *furreigners* from the cut of our coats. He began to talk hostile, and was, as they brag in the timber districts, twenty foot in the clear, without limb, knot, windshake, or woodpecker hole. To appease him, I agreed, if the stakeholder could not be found, to be responsible for his stake. He very industriously made proclamation for the young man with the wall-eyed horse, and being informed that he had *done gone* three hours ago, he claimed of me, and I had to shell out.

Feeling somewhat worsted by this transaction, I concluded I would look up my other bets. Mr. Wash I did not see, and concluded he had retired; I found the stakeholder that assisted about the bar, and claimed my five dollars on the draw race; to my surprise I learned he had given up the stakes. Having been previously irritated, I made some severe remarks, to all of which he replied in perfect good temper, and assured me he was the most punctilious person in the world about such matters, and that it was his invariable rule never to give up stakes except by the direction of some of the judges, and called up proof of his having declined delivering the stakes until he and the claimant went to old screw-eye; and he decided I had lost. This seemed to put the matter out of dispute so far as he was concerned, but thinking I would make an appeal to my opponent, I inquired if he knew him. He satisfied me, by assuring me he did not *know him from a side of sole leather.*

I left the course, and on returning next morning, I looked out for Mr. Wash; I discovered him drinking, and offering large bets; he saw me plainly, but affected a perfect forgetfulness, and did not recognise me. After waiting some time, and finding he would not address me, I approached him, and requested an opportunity of speaking to him apart. Mr. Wash instantly accompanied me, and began telling me he had got in a scrape, and had never in his life been in such a fix. Perceiving what he was at, I concluded to take the whip-hand of him, and observed—"Mr. Wash, if you design to intimate by your preliminary remarks that you cannot return to me my own money, staked in your hands, I must say I consider such conduct extremely ungentlemanly." Upon this he whipped out a spring-back dirk knife, nine inches in the blade, and whetted to cut a hair, stepped off, picked up a piece of cedar, and commenced whittling. "Now, stranger," says he, "I would not advise any man to try to run over me, for I ask no man any odds further than civility; I consider myself as honest a man as any in Harris county, Kentucky; but I'll tell you, stranger, exactly how it happened: you see, when you offered to bet on the sorrel, I was out of soap, but it was too good a chance to let slip, as I was dead sure Popcorn would win; and if he had won, you know, of course it made no difference to you whether I had a stake or not. Well, it was none of my business to hunt you up, so I went to town last night to the confectionary, [a whisky shop in a log pen fourteen feet square,] and I thought I'd make a rise on chuck-a-luck, but you *prehaps* never saw such a run of luck; everywhere I touched was *pizen*, and I came out of the *leetle end* of the horn; but I'll tell you what, I'm a man that always stands up to my fodder, rack or no rack; so, as you don't want the money, I'll negotiate to suit you exactly; I'll give you my *dubisary:* I don't know that I can pay it this year, unless the *crap* of hemp turns out well; but if I can't this year, I will next year probably; and I'll tell you exactly my principle—if a man waits with me like a gentleman, I'm sure to pay him when I'm ready; but if a man tries to bear down on me and make me pay whether or no, you see it is his own look out, and he'll see sights before he gets his money." My respect for Mr. Wash's dirk-knife, together with my perceiving there was nothing else to be had, induced me to express my entire satisfaction with Mr. Wash's *dubisary*, hoping at the same time that at least *enough* of hemp would grow that year. He proposed that I should let him have five dollars more for a stake, but on my declining, he said, "Well, there is no harm in mentioning it." He went to the bar, borrowed pen and ink, and presently returned with a splendid specimen of caligraphy to the following effect:—

State of Kentucky, Jessamine county. } Due Dempsey, the just and lawful sum of ten dollars, for value received, payable on the 26th day of December, 1836 or 1837, or any time after that I am able to discharge the same. As witness my hand and seal, this 30th day of May, 1836.

GEORGE WASHINGTON BRIGGS. { SEAL }

I wish you would try Wall street with this paper, as I wish to cash it; but I'll run a mile before I wait for a quarter race again.

A SHARK STORY.

BY "J. CYPRESS, JR.," THE LATE WM. P. HAWES, ESQ. OF NEW YORK.

No native writer of his age, probably, ever acquired so enviable a reputation at home and abroad, as was universally accorded to the late lamented Wm. P. Hawes, Esq., of New York, whose sketches, under the signature of "J. Cypress, Jr.," were everywhere sought for, and read with the highest degree of interest. A collection of his contributions to the press was published two or three years since, under the title of "*Country Scenes and Sundry Sketches*," (edited by "Frank Forester,") to which attention is invited as being one of the most humorous original works in the language. The capital story subjoined will give a very good idea of his style.

"Well, gentlemen, I'll go ahead, if you say so. Here's the story. It is true, upon my honour, from beginning to end—every word of it. I once crossed over to Faulkner's island to fish for *tautaugs*, as the north-side people call black fish, on the reefs hard by, in the Long Island Sound. Tim Titus (who died of the dropsy down at Shinnecock point, last spring) lived there then. Tim was a right good fellow, only he drank rather too much.

"It was during the latter part of July; the sharks and the dog-fish had just began to spoil sport. When Tim told me about the sharks, I resolved to go prepared to entertain these aquatic savages with all becoming attention and regard, if there should chance to be any interloping about our fishing ground. So, we rigged out a set of extra large hooks, and shipped some ropeyarn and steel chain, an axe, a couple of clubs, and an old harpoon, in addition to our ordinary equipments, and off we started. We threw out our anchor at half-ebb tide, and took some thumping large fish: two of them weighed thirteen pounds—so you may judge. The reef where we lay was about half a mile from the island, and, perhaps, a mile from the Connecticut shore. We floated there, very quietly, throwing out and hauling in, until the breaking of my line, with a sudden and severe jerk, informed me that the sea attorneys were in waiting, down stairs; and we accordingly prepared to give them a retainer. A salt pork cloak upon one of our magnum hooks forthwith engaged one of the gentlemen in our service. We got him alongside, and by dint of piercing, and thrusting, and banging, we accomplished a most exciting and merry murder. We had business enough of the kind to keep us employed until near low water. By this time, the sharks had all cleared out, and the black fish were biting again; the rock began to make its appearance above the water, and in a little while its hard bald head was entirely dry. Tim now proposed to set me out upon the rock, while he rowed ashore to get the jug, which, strange to say, we had left at the house. I assented to this proposition; first, because I began to feel the effects of the sun upon my tongue, and needed something to take, by the way of medicine; and secondly, because the rock was a favourite spot for rod and reel, and famous for luck: so I took my *traps*, and a box of bait, and jumped upon my new station. Tim made for the island.

"Not many men would willingly have been left upon a little barren reef that was covered by every flow of the tide, in the midst of a waste of waters, at such a distance from the shore, even with an assurance from a companion more to be depended upon than mine, that he would return immediately and take him off. But some how or other, the excitement of my sport was so high, and the romance of the situation was so delightful, that I thought of nothing else but the prospect of my fun, and the contemplation of the novelty and beauty of the scene. It was a mild, pleasant afternoon, in harvest time. The sky was clear and pure. The deep blue sound, heaving all around me, was studded with craft of all descriptions and dimensions, from the dipping sail-boat to the rolling merchantman, sinking and rising like sea-birds sporting with their white wings in the surge. The grain and grass on the neighbouring farms were gold and green, and gracefully they bent obeisance to a gently breathing south-wester. Farther off, the high upland, and the distant coast, gave a dim relief to the prominent features of the landscape, and seemed the rich but dusky frame of a brilliant fairy picture. Then, how still it was! not a sound could be heard, except the occasional rustling of my own motion, and the water beating against the sides, or gurgling in the fissures of the rock, or except now and then the cry of a solitary saucy gull, who would come out of his way in the firmament, to see what I was doing without a boat, all alone, in the middle of the sound; and who would hover, and cry, and chatter, and make two or three circling swoops and dashes at me, and then, after having satisfied his curiosity, glide away in search of some other food to scream at.

"I soon became half indolent, and quite indifferent about fishing; so I stretched myself out at full length upon the rock, and gave myself up to the luxury of looking and thinking. The divine exercise soon put me fast asleep. I dreamed away a couple of hours, and longer might have dreamed, but for a tired fish-hawk who chose to make my head his resting place, and who waked and started me to my feet.

"'Where is Tim Titus?' I muttered to myself, as I strained my eyes over the now darkened water. But none was near me to answer that interesting question, and nothing was to be seen of either Tim or his boat. 'He should have been here long ere this,' thought I, 'and he promised faithfully not to stay long—could he have forgotten? or has he paid too much devotion to the jug?'

"I began to feel uneasy, for the tide was rising fast, and soon would cover the top of the rock, and high water-mark was at least a foot above my head. I buttoned up my coat, for either the coming coolness of the evening, or else my growing apprehensions, had set me trembling and chattering most painfully. I braced my nerves, and set my teeth, and tried to hum 'Begone, dull care,' keeping time with my fists upon my thighs. But what music! what melancholy merriment! I started and shuddered at the doleful sound of my own voice. I am not naturally a coward; but I should like to know the man who would not, in such a situation, be alarmed. It is a cruel death to die to be merely drowned, and to go through the ordinary common-places of suffocation; but to see your death gradually rising to your eyes, to feel the water rising, inch by inch, upon your shivering sides, and to anticipate the certainly coming, choking struggle for your last breath, when, with the gurgling sound of an overflowing brook taking a new direction, the cold brine pours into mouth, ears, and nostrils, usurping the seat and avenues of health and life, and, with gradual flow, stifling—smothering—suffocating! It were better to die a thousand common deaths.

"This is one of the instances in which, it must be admitted, salt water is not a pleasant subject of contemplation. However, the rock was not yet covered, and hope, blessed hope, stuck faithfully by me. To beguile, if possible, the weary time, I put on a bait, and threw out for fish. I was sooner successful than I could have wished to be, for hardly had my line struck the water, before the hook was swallowed, and my rod was bent with the dead hard pull of a twelve foot shark. I let him run about fifty yards, and then reeled up. He appeared not at all alarmed, and I could scarcely feel him bear upon my fine hair line. He followed the pull gently and unresisting, came up to the rock, laid his nose upon its side, and looked up into my face, not as if utterly unconcerned, but with a sort of quizzical impudence, as though he perfectly understood the precarious nature of my situation. The conduct of my captive renewed and increased my alarm. And well it might; for the tide was now running over a corner of the rock behind me, and a small stream rushed through a cleft, or fissure, by my side, and formed a puddle at my very feet. I broke my hook out of the monster's mouth, and leaned upon my rod for support.

"'Where is Tim Titus?'—I cried aloud—'Curse on the drunken vagabond! Will he never come?'

"My ejaculations did no good. No Timothy appeared. It became evident that I must prepare for drowning, or for action. The reef was completely covered, and the water was above the soles of my feet. I was not much of a swimmer, and as to ever reaching the island, I could not even hope for that. However, there was no alternative, and I tried to encourage myself, by reflecting that necessity was the mother of invention, and that desperation will sometimes insure success. Besides, too, I considered and took comfort from the thought that I could wait for Tim, so long as I had a foothold, and then commit myself to the uncertain strength of my arms and legs for salvation. So I turned my bait-box upside down, and mounting upon that, endeavoured to comfort my spirits, and to be courageous, but submissive to my fate. I thought of death, and what it might bring with it, and I tried to repent of the multiplied iniquities of my almost wasted life; but I found that that was no place for a sinner to settle his accounts. Wretched soul, pray I could not.

"The water had not got above my ankles, when, to my inexpressible joy, I saw a sloop bending down towards me, with the evident intention of picking me up. No man can imagine what were the sensations of gratitude which filled my bosom at that moment.

"When she got within a hundred yards of the reef, I sung out to the man at the helm to luff up, and lie by, and lower the boat; but, to my amazement, I could get no-reply, nor notice of my request. I entreated them, for the love of heaven, to take me off; and I promised, I know not what rewards, that were entirely beyond my power of bestowal. But the brutal wretch of a captain, muttering something to the effect of 'that he hadn't time to stop,' and giving me the kind and sensible advice to pull off my coat and swim ashore, put the helm hard down, and away bore the sloop on the other tack.

"'Heartless villain!'—I shrieked out, in the torture of my disappointment; 'may God reward your inhumanity.' The crew answered my prayer with a coarse, loud laugh; and the cook asked me through a speaking trumpet, 'If I was not afraid of catching cold.'—The black rascal!

"It now was time to strip; for my knees felt the cool tide, and the wind, dying away, left a heavy swell, that swayed and shook the box upon which I was mounted, so that I had occasionally to stoop, and paddle with my hands against the water, in order to preserve my perpendicular. The setting sun sent his almost horizontal streams of fire across the dark waters, making them gloomy and terrific, by the contrast of his amber and purple glories.

"Something glided by me in the water, and then made a sudden halt. I looked upon the black mass, and, as my eye ran along its dark outline, I saw, with horror, that it was a shark; the identical monster out of whose mouth I had just broken my hook. He was fishing now for me, and was evidently only waiting for the tide to rise high enough above the rock, to glut at once his hunger and revenge. As the water continued to mount above my knees, he seemed to grow more hungry and familiar. At last, he made a desperate dash, and, approaching within an inch of my legs, turned upon his back, and opened his huge jaws for an attack. With desperate strength, I thrust the end of my rod violently at his mouth; and the brass head, ringing against his teeth, threw him back into the deep current, and I lost sight of him entirely. This, however,

A SHARK STORY.

"As I looked around me to see what had become of the robbers, I counted one, two, three, yes, up to twelve, successively, of the largest sharks I ever saw!"—*Page* 33.

was but a momentary repulse; for in the next minute he was close behind my back, and pulling at the skirts of my fustian coat, which hung dipping into the water. I leaned forward hastily, and endeavoured to extricate myself from the dangerous grasp; but the monster's teeth were too firmly set, and his immense strength nearly drew me over. So, down flew my rod, and off went my jacket, devoted peace-offerings to my voracious visiter.

"In an instant, the waves all round me were lashed into froth and foam. No sooner was my poor old sporting friend drawn under the surface, than it was fought for by at least a dozen enormous combatants! The battle raged upon every side. High black fins rushed now here, now there, and long, strong tails scattered sleet and froth, and the brine was thrown up in jets, and eddied, and curled, and fell, and swelled, like a whirlpool in Hell-gate.

"Of no long duration, however, was this fishy tourney. It seemed soon to be discovered that the prize contended for contained nothing edible but cheese and crackers, and no flesh; and as its mutilated fragments rose to the surface, the waves subsided into their former smooth condition. Not till then did I experience the real terrors of my situation. As I looked around me to see what had become of the robbers, I counted one, two, three, yes, up to twelve, successively, of the largest sharks I ever saw, floating in a circle around me, like divergent rays, all mathematically equidistant from the rock, and from each other; each perfectly motionless, and with his gloating, fiery eye, fixed full and fierce upon me. Basilisks and rattlesnakes! how the fire of their steady eyes entered into my heart! I was the centre of a circle, whose radii were sharks! I was the unsprung, or rather *unchewed* game, at which a pack of hunting sea-dogs were making a dead point!

"There was one old fellow, that kept within the circumference of the circle. He seemed to be a sort of captain, or leader of the band; or, rather, he acted as the coroner for the other twelve of the inquisition, that were summoned to sit on, and eat up my body. He glided around and about, and every now and then would stop, and touch his nose against some one of his comrades, and seem to consult, or to give instructions as to the time and mode of operation. Occasionally, he would skull himself up towards me, and examine the condition of my flesh, and then again glide back, and rejoin the troupe, and flap his tail, and have another confabulation. The old rascal had, no doubt, been out into the highways and byways, and collected this company of his friends and kin-fish, and invited them to supper. I must confess, that horribly as I felt, I could not help but think of a tea party, of demure old maids, sitting in a solemn circle, with their skinny hands in their laps, licking their expecting lips, while their hostess bustles about in the important functions of her preparations. With what an eye have I seen such appurtenances of humanity survey the location and adjustment of some especial condiment, which is about to be submitted to criticism and consumption.

"My sensations began to be, now, most exquisite indeed; but I will not attempt to describe them. I was neither hot nor cold, frightened nor composed; but I had a combination of all kinds of feelings and emotions. The present, past, future, heaven, earth, my father and mother, a little girl I knew once, and the sharks, were all confusedly mixed up together, and swelled my crazy brain almost to bursting. I cried, and laughed, and spouted, and screamed for Tim Titus. In a fit of most wise madness, I opened my broad-bladed fishing knife, and waved it around my head with an air of defiance. As the tide continued to rise, my extravagance of madness mounted. At one time, I became persuaded that my tide-waiters were reasonable beings, who might be talked into mercy and humanity, if a body could only hit upon the right text. So, I bowed, and gesticulated, and threw out my hands, and talked to them, as friends, and brothers, members of my family, cousins, uncles, aunts, people waiting to have their bills paid;—I scolded them as my servants; I abused them as duns; I implored them as jurymen sitting on the question of my life; I congratulated, and flattered them as my comrades upon some glorious enterprise; I sung and ranted to them, now as an actor in a play-house, and now as an elder at a camp-meeting; in one moment, roaring,

> 'On this cold flinty rock I will lay down my head,'—

and in the next, giving out to my attentive hearers for singing, a hymn of Dr. Watts so admirably appropriate to the occasion,

> 'On slippery rocks I see them stand,
> While fiery billows roll below.'

"What said I, what did I not say! Prose and poetry, scripture and drama, romance and ratiocination—out it came. '*Quamdiu, Catalina, nostra patientia abutere?*'—I sung out to the old captain, to begin with—'My brave associates, partners of my toil,'—so ran the strain. 'On which side soever I turn my eyes,'—'Gentlemen of the jury,'—'I come not here to steal away your hearts,'—'You are not wood, you are not stones, but'—'Hah!'—'Begin, ye tormentors, your tortures are vain,'—'Good friends, sweet friends, let me not stir you up to any sudden flood,'—'The angry flood that lashed her groaning sides,'—'Ladies and gentlemen,'—'My very noble and approved good masters,'—'Avaunt! and quit my sight; let the earth hide ye,'—'Lie lightly on his head, O earth!'—'O! heaven and earth! that it should come to this,'—'The torrent roared, and we did buffet it with lusty sinews, stemming it aside and oaring it with hearts of controversy,'—'Give me some drink, Titinius,'—'Drink, boys, drink, and drown dull sorrow,'—'For liquor it doth roll such comfort to the soul,'—'Romans, countrymen and lovers, hear me for my cause, and be silent that you may hear,'—'Fellow citizens, assembled as we are upon this interesting occasion, impressed with the truth and beauty,'—'Isle of beauty, fare thee well,'—'The quality of mercy is not strained,'—'Magna veritas et prevalebit,'—'Truth is potent, and'—'Most potent, grave, and reverend seigniors,—

'Oh, now you weep, and I perceive you feel
The dint of pity; these are gracious drops.
Kind souls! what! weep you when you but behold
Our Cæsar's vesture wounded,'—

Ha! ha! ha!—and I broke out in a fit of most horrible laughter, as I thought of the mincemeat particles of my lacerated jacket.

"In the mean time, the water had got well up towards my shoulders, and while I was shaking and vibrating upon my uncertain foot-hold, I felt the cold nose of the captain of the band snubbing against my side. Desperately, and without a definite object, I struck my knife at one of his eyes, and, by some singular fortune, cut it out clean from the socket. The shark darted back, and halted. In an instant, hope and reason came to my relief; and it occurred to me, that if I could only blind the monster, I might yet escape. Accordingly, I stood ready for the next attack. The loss of an eye did not seem to affect him much, for, after shaking his head once or twice, he came up to me again, and when he was about half an inch off, turned upon his back. This was the critical moment. With a most unaccountable presence of mind, I laid hold of his nose with my left hand, and with my right scooped out his remaining organ of vision. He opened his big mouth, and champed his long teeth at me, in despair. But it was all over with him. I raised my right foot and gave him a hard shove, and he glided off into deep water, and went to the bottom.

"Well, gentlemen, I suppose you'd think it a hard story, but its none the less a fact, that I served every remaining one of those nineteen sharks in the same fashion. They all came up to me, one by one, regularly and in order, and I scooped their eyes out, and gave them a shove, and they went off into deep water, just like so many lambs. By the time I had scooped out and blinded a couple of dozen of them, they began to seem so scarce that I thought I would swim for the island, and fight the rest for fun, on the way; but just then, Tim Titus hove in sight, and it had got to be almost dark, and I concluded to get aboard and rest myself."

LANTY OLIPHANT IN COURT.

BY MAJ. KELLY, OF LOUISIANA.

The writer of the diverting sketch annexed has taken leave of his editorial sanctum, and "gone to the wars;" in other words, to Mexico, where, we trust, he will render as good an account of himself as he has of "LANTY OLIPHANT."

LAWYERS allege that there are four classes of witnesses —those who prove too much, those who prove too little, those of a totally negative character, and those of no character at all, who will prove any thing. We have a case in point.

Far, very far away from the tall Blue mountains, at a little place called Sodom, there were upon a time three neighbours called in as arbitrators to settle a point, relative to some stolen chickens, in dispute between one Lot Corson and a "hard case" called Emanuel Allen, better known thereabout as King of the Marsh.

"Mister Constable," said one of the demi-judicials, "now call the principal witness."

"Lanty Oliphant! Lanty Olip-h-a-n-t!" bawled Dogberry. "Mosey in and be swore."

In obedience to this summons, little Lanty, whose bottle had usurped the place in his affections commonly assigned to soap and water, waddled up, and was qualified, deprecating by a look the necessity of such a useless ceremony among gentlemen.

"Mister Oliphant, you are now swore. Do you know the value of an oath?" asked the senior of the board.

"Doesn't I!" rejoined Lanty, with a wink at a by-stander. "Four bushel of weight wheat, the old score wiped off, and licker for the hul day throw'd in."

This matter-of-fact answer met a severe frown from the man with the red ribbon round his hat.

"Well, Mister Oliphant," continued the senior, "tell all you know about this here case. Bill M——k, *shoo* your dog off that d—d old sow."

Lanty here testified. "Feelin' a sort of outish t'other day, ses I to the old woman, ses I, I'll jist walk over to Lot's and take a nipper or two this mornin', ses I. It'll take the wind off my stomach sorter, ses I. Then the old woman's feathers riz, they did, like a porkypine's bristles, and ses she, Lanty, says she, if you'd on'y airn more bread and meat, and drink less whisky, you would'nt have wind on your stomach. Suse, ses I, this is one of my resarved rights, and I goes agin home industry, ses I, sort o' laughin' out o' the wrong side o' my mouth. 'Resarved rights or desarved wrongs,' ses her, 'you'r always a drinkin' and talkin' politics when you orter be at work, and there's never nothin' to eat in the house.' Well, as I was agoin over to Lot's jist fernent where the fence *was*, ses I to myself, ses I, if there is'nt the old King's critters in my corn field, so I'll jist go and tell him on't. When I gets there, Good mornin', Lanty, ses he. Good mornin', old hoss, ses I, and when I went in, there was a pot on the fire a cookin', with a *great big speckled rooster* in it."

"Mister Oliphant!" here interposed one of the arbitrators. "Remember that you are on oath. How do you know that the chicken in the pot was 'a big speckled rooster?'"

"'Kase I *seed the feathers at the woodpile!*" promptly responded Lanty, who then continued:

"Well, when I gits to Lot's, Good mornin', Lot, ses I. Good mornin', Lanty, ses he. You didn't see nothin' no where of nar' a big speckled rooster that didn't belong to nobody, did you? ses he. Didn't I? ses I. Come, Lanty, ses he, let's take a nipper, ses he; and then I up and tells him all about it."

"Had Mr. Allen no chickens of his own?" asked the senior.

"Sartin'," rejoined Lanty; "but there warn't a rooster in the crowd. They was *all layin' hens!*"

"Well," inquired another of the referees, "how many of these hens had Mr. Allen?"

This question fairly "stump'd" Lanty for a moment, but he quickly answered:

"Why, with what was there, and what wasn't there, counting little and big, spring chickens and all, *there was forty odd*, EXACTLY!"

No further questions were put to this witness!

BILL MORSE ON THE CITY TAXES.

BY "BAGGS," OF BOSTON, MASS.

The following sketch is the first of a series which have appeared in the "Spirit of the Times," from the pen of a young gentleman of Boston, from whom "great things" are expected "one of these days."

Some time ago, long before the "Boundary Question" was settled, there lived upon the extreme frontiers of Maine a young man ycleped "Bill Morse." He supported a primitive sort of establishment, and his whole circle of acquaintance consisted of some half a dozen half-civilized individuals, residing in the vicinity. His principal occupations were killing venison and felling trees; and reading and writing were accomplishments to which Bill laid no claim.

In the course of time, however, a rich relation—a Southern planter probably—happened to leave this world for a better, and, fortunately for Bill, left no will behind him. By a curious and intricate course of legal proceedings and without any interference on his part, Bill Morse found himself a wealthy man. The "gentleman of the green bag" who travelled down to impart this information, conducted Bill to Bangor, and then having appointed himself Bill's agent, left things to themselves. The young gentleman came out in due time in very bold colours, and having always plenty of money at his disposal, enjoyed himself without stint.

Among other rents through which his surplus cash

formed a ready passage, was a large *tax*, which in the course of the year was assessed upon him. The bill was presented, but for the life of him, Bill couldn't make out its meaning. After some minutes' attentive scrutiny of the article, he proceeded to the landlord of the hotel where he visited.

"I say, landlord," said he, "what's this?"

"That, Mr. Morse," answered the landlord, casting his eyes over the paper, "is a tax bill."

"A tax bill," murmured Bill, regarding it with an inquisitive glance—"yes, but what's that?"

"Why," answered the landlord smiling, "it's your proportion of the expenses of the city."

"My proportion!" said Bill. "What, does every one pay?"

"Certainly," replied the landlord, "every one who can afford it."

"Oh, I can *afford* it," said Bill, who was here touched upon a tender point; "I'll send and have it paid."

The bill was settled, and in proper time a second made its appearance. Bill hastened to the landlord. "Look here," said he in astonishment, "here's another of them tax bills!"

"Of course," replied the landlord; "they come once a year."

"The devil they do," cried Bill; "so the city goes into debt every year, does it?"

"Regularly," said the landlord; "it can't be helped."

"Well, then, damn me!" cried Bill in a high passion, "*if the city hasn't got any better business to do than to keep on running up debts for me to help her out because I did it once, she'll find herself extensively mistaken*—I'll see her d—d before I give her another red cent!"

ANCE VEASY'S FIGHT WITH REUB. SESSIONS.

BY "AZUL," OF MISSISSIPPI.

The writer of the "good 'un" subjoined is a new correspondent of the "Spirit of the Times," with whose name and local habitation the editor is as familiar as he is with the veritable man-in-the-moon. He promises to be a valuable acquisition to the number of our native humorists.

"ARE you in favour of Biennial Sessions of the legislature?" asked a manager of an election in Alabama, of a voter.

"Who?" says the voter, whose name was ANCE VEASY, and withal, tolerably green.

"Are you in favour of Biennial Sessions of the legislature, Sir?"

"Benial Sessions! I don't know him. Is he any kin to *Reub.* Sessions? Sir; ef he is I'll bed—d ef you ketch me a votin fur him! You never hearn me tell about that fite I had long wid Reub. Sessions, up in Shelby, did you?"

"Never mind your fights, now, Mr. Veasy: answer yea or nay."

"I dosen't know what you mean by your ya and na's, but I'll be *dod rotted* ef I vote fur enny uv the Sessions family, no how you can fix it! Bah! *Benial* Sessions, indeed! jest as much fit fur Guvnur as h–ll is fur a ice-house!"

"Are you in favour of the removal of the State House, Mr. Veasy?"

"Well I wonder ef tha is 'gwine too move the State House agin? Why tha moved it only two or three years ago to Wetumpka. I don't see no use of thar movin it enny more—I think it's in a very good place myself, I does them, punkins!"

"You are thinking of the Penitentiary, Mr. Veasy. It's the State House they wish to move!"

"Well, it taint nothin too me whether tha move it or not, so I won't vote for it, nor Benial Sessions nuther!"

Several now pressed around Ance to get him to tell about his fight with Reub. Sessions, up in Shelby. He said he would come to these terms. They were to give him a good drink of whisky, and he was to give them the story. They agreed to it, and gave him the whisky, and he commenced.

"You see a passel uv us fellers made up a camp-hunt betwixt us, and Reub., he went with us, but he never tuck no gun, kase he was so infurnal lazy that he woodn't even take a stand and watch fur deer. He jest went along to eat wenzon and to help the fellers cook. Well, the fust evenin we were out, we killed a mitey fine tow hed deer, and we fotch him in an cooked wun quarter fur supper. Reub. ett 'bout half uv that quarter; and arter we went sleep, and 'bout midnite I got awake and razed up, and thar wuz Reub. eatin away like he was paid fur it. I never sed nuthin, but laid down and went too sleep: an 'bout daylite I waked up and begun too get reddy too go out and kill sum game, and I'll be dod durned ef Reub. wuzn't eatin away still, or ruther, pickin the bones, fur he had ett up all the hole deer an wuz

"We fit round and round about the barrels and boxes 'bout half an hour."—
Page 45.

pickin the bones. Git up, you holler-legged, pot-gutted, turkey-buzzard, sez I, and make tracks fur home jest as fast as you kin poot wun leg afore the tuther! and I tuck the feller side uv the hed with my fist and sorter turned him over; but he got up pooty soon and done sum uv the tallest kind uv walking fur home.

"About two or three weeks after the hunt that we wuz all at Simmon's grocery, on the Montevallo road, an I wuz tellin the fellars 'bout Reub.'s eatin a hole tow deer an nawin the bones besides, an the feller got rite ashy 'bout it, but I didn't mind him nor never paid no 'tention to him, till he bucked up too me an give me a feller rite under the ear, an I tell ye it made my hed kinder dizzy. When he gin me the fust lick it made me sorter mad, but I woodn't a minded ef he hadn't kept pilin on the agony 'bout my ears and smeller. When I did git my *Norf Carliner* up, the way I pitched it in too him was a caution to mules. We fit round and round about the barrels an boxes 'bout half an hour, when I got his hed under my arm an I made him squeal immediantly, but I wuzn't gwine too let him off without givin him sumthin too 'member Ance Veasy by, an I tell you fellers, I natally peeled the skin off his face an then I turned him loose. He tuck up his hat, an when I sorter turned my back too him, he picked up an ole axe helve an gin me a wipe aside the hed that laid me cole fur a while I tell you. But I picked myself up an started sorter arter him, but he wuz on his hoss an fast banishing out uv site over the hill.

"The sheriff cum an tuck me up an tried me for trying to kill, but tha found me requitted, an let me loose, coz I gin mvself up. But Reub., he run away, kase he thort how he had killed me, an he stayed away two or three months; but wen he heerd as how I wuzn't ded, he cum back an the sheriff nabbed him an carried him too the Cort-house, an tride him fur salt and batter an murder with intent too kill. Tha found him requitted of murder, but tha found him gilty uv salt an batter. I didn't see enny salt in the fite, but thar wuz sum batterin done, but I done all the batterin myself, except wot he done with the axe helve. I don't think the feller wot tride him done fair by him, kase tha kused him uv 'tackin me with pistols an knives, but thar wuzn't narry pistol nor knife on the ground at the time. Enny how the Judge says he,

"'Mr. Sessions, the jury has found you gilty uv salt an batter, an you must go too jail fur wun munth an pay twenty-five dollars besides.'

"'I don't keer ef you make it two munths, by —!' says Reub.

"'Fine him ten dollars, Mr. Sheriff, fur swarin in Cort.'

"'I don't keer ef you make it twenty dollars, by —!' says Reub.

"'Fine him twenty dollars and three munths imprisonment, Mr. Sheriff,' says the Judge.

"That made Reub. stap cussin in the Cort-House, I tell you, an the Sheriff tuck him off too jail and locked him up, an he had too stay thar four munths by himself.

"I had a fite wunst over on the Cahawba river, with a Tennesee wagoner's dog—did you ever hear me tell 'bout it? but never mind now, fellers, I'm gitten mity dry, an I have too wate until I git a nuther horn, an I don't keer who pays fur it, I don't."

THE FASTEST FUNERAL ON RECORD.

BY F. A. DURIVAGE, ESQ., OF BOSTON, MASS.

Under the well-known signature of "The Old 'Un," in the "Spirit of the Times," Mr. Durivage has acquired the highest reputation. His "Ghost of the Eleven Strike," and other original comic sketches, have been read with delight by thousands. He is now the editor of the Boston "Weekly Symbol"—a *very* "Odd Fellow's" paper, which he conducts with signal ability.

"Hurrah! hurrah! the dead ride fast—
Dost fear to ride with me?"—*Burger's Leonora.*

"This fellow has no feeling of his business."—*Hamlet.*

Mr. P.—I HAD just crossed the long bridge leading from Boston to Cambridgeport, and was plodding my dusty way on foot through that not very agreeable suburb, on a sultry afternoon in July, with a very creditable thunder-cloud coming up in my rear, when a stout elderly gentleman, with a mulberry face, a brown coat, and pepper-and-salt smalls, reined up his nag, and after learning that I was bound for Old Cambridge, politely invited me to take a seat beside him in the little sort of tax-cart he was driving. Nothing loath, I consented, and we were soon *en route.* The mare he drove was a very peculiar animal. She had few good points to the eye, being heavy-bodied, hammer-headed, thin in the shoulders, bald-faced, and rejoicing in a little stump of a tail which was almost entirely innocent of hair. But there were "lots of muscle," as Major Longbow says, in her hind quarters.

"She aint no Wenus, Sir," said my new acquaintance, pointing with his whip to the object of my scrutiny —"but handsome is as handsome does. Them's my sentiments. She's a rum 'un to look at, but a good 'un to go."

"Indeed?"

"Yes, *Sir!* That there mare, sir, has made good time—I may say, *very* good time before the hearse."

"Before the hearse?"

"Before the hearse! S'pose you never heard of *burying a man on time!* I'm a sexton, sir, and undertaker—Jack Crossbones, at your service—'Daddy Crossbones' they call me at Porter's."

"Ah! I understand. Your mare ran away with the hearse."

"Ran away! A child could hold her. Oh! yes, of course she ran away," added the old gentleman, looking full in my face with a very quizzical expression, and putting the fore finger of his right hand on the right side of his party-coloured proboscis.

"My dear Sir," said I, "you have excited my curiosity amazingly, and I should esteem it as a particular favour if you would be a little less oracular and a little more explicit."

"I don't know as I'd ought to tell you," said my new acquaintance very slowly and tantalizingly. "If you was one of these here writing chaps, you might poke it in the 'Spirit of the Times,' and then it would be all day with me. But I don't care if I do make a clean breast of it. Honour bright, you know."

"Of course."

"Well, then, I live a piece up beyond Old Cambridge—you can see our steeple off on a hill to the right, when we get a little further. Well, one day, I had a customer—(he was carried off by the typhus)—which had to be toted into town—cause why? he had a vault there. So I rubbed down the old mare and put her in the fills. Ah! Sir! that critter knows as much as an Injun, and more than a Nigger. She's as sober 'as be d—d' when she get's the shop—that's what I call the hearse—behind her. You would not think she was a three-minute nag, to look at her. Well, sir, as luck would have it, by a sort of providential inspiration, the day before, I'd took off the old wooden springs and set the body on elliptics. For I thought it a hard case that a gentleman who'd been riding easy all his life, should go to his grave on wooden springs. Ah! I deal well by my customers. I thought of patent boxes to the wheels, but *I* couldn't afford it, and the parish are desperate stingy.

"Well, I got him in, and led off the string—fourteen hacks, and a dearbourn wagon at the tail of the funeral. We made a fine show. As luck would have it, just as we came abreast of Porter's, out slides that eternal torment, BILL SIKES, in his new trotting sulky, with the brown horse that he bought for a fast crab, and *is* mighty good for a rush, but hain't got nigh so much bottom as the mare. Bill's light weight, and his sulky's a mere feather. Well, sir, Bill came up alongside, and walked his horse a bit. He looked at the mare and then at me, and then he winked. Then he looked at his nag and put his tongue in his cheek, and winked. I looked straight ahead, and only said to myself, 'Cuss you, Bill Sikes.' By and by, he let his horse slide. He travelled about a hundred yards, and then held up till I came abreast, and then he winked and bantered me again. It was d—d aggravatin'. Says I to myself, says I—'that's twice you've done it, my buzzum friend and sweet-scented shrub—but you doesn't do that 'ere again.' The third time he bantered me, I let him have it. It was only saying 'Scat you brute,' and she was off—that mare. He had all the odds, you know, for I was toting a two hundred pounder, and he ought to have beat me like breaking sticks, now hadn't he? He had me at the first brush, for I told you the brown horse was a mighty fast one for a little ways. But soon I lapped him. I had no whip, and he could use his string—but he had his hands full. Side by side, away we went. Rattle-te-bang! crack! abuz! thump! And I afraid of losing my customer on the road. But I was more afraid of losing the race. The reputation of the old mare was at a stake, and I swore she should have a fair chance. We went so fast that the posts and rails by the road side looked like a log fence. The old church and the new one, and the colleges, spun past like Merry Andrews. The hackmen did not know what the —— was to pay, and, afraid of not being in at the death, they put the string onto their teams, and came clattering on behind as if Satan had kicked 'em on eend. Some of the mourners was sporting characters, and they craned out of the carriage windows and waved their handkerchiefs. The President of Harvard

College himself, inspired by the scene, took off his square tile as I passed his house, and waving it three times round his head, cried, 'Go it, Boots!' It *is* a fact. And I beat him, sir! I beat him, in three miles, a hundred rods. He gin it up, sir, in despair."

"His horse was off his feed for a week, and when he took to corn again he wasn't worth a straw. It was acknowledged on all hands to be the fastest funeral on record, though I say it as shouldn't. I'm an undertaker, sir, and I never yet was overtaken."

On subsequent inquiry at Porter's, where the sporting sexton left me, I found that his story was strictly true in all the main particulars. A terrible rumpus was kicked up about the race, but Crossbones swore lustily that the mare had run away—that he had sawed away two inches of her lip in trying to hold her up, and that he could not have done otherwise, unless he had run her into a fence and spilled his "customer" into the ditch. If any one expects to die anywhere near the sexton's *diggings*, I can assure them that the jolly old boy is still alive and kicking, the very "Ace of Hearts" and "Jack of Spades," and that now both patent boxes and elliptic springs render his professional conveyance the easiest running thing on the road.

GOING TO BED BEFORE A YOUNG LADY.

BY JUDGE DOUGLASS, OF ILLINOIS.

Next to judge "Horse Allen," of Missouri, Judge Douglass, of Illinois, is decidedly the most original and amusing member of the western bar—or *we* are no judge.

As I was saying, ten years ago, Judge Douglass, of Illinois, was a beardless youth of twenty years of age, freshly come amongst the people of the "Sucker State," with an air about him suspiciously redolent of Yankee-land. A mere youthful adventurer amongst those "quare" Suckers—one would deem the position embarrassing. Not so with the judge; he had come on business. A political fortune was to be made, and no time lost. He was about launching on the sea of popular favour, and he commenced a general coast survey the day he arrived. He soon made himself District Attorney, member of the Legislature, Register of the U. S. Land Office, Secretary of State, and Judge of the Supreme Court.

"How do you adapt yourself," said I, "Judge, to the people? How did you 'naturalize' yourself, as it were?"

"Oh, nothing easier; you see I like it. It's democratic. But it did come awkward at first. You know I am, or rather was, bashful to rather a painful degree. Well, now, nine-tenths of my constituents despise luxuries, and have no such thing as a second room in their houses. In beating up for votes, I live with my constituents, eat with my constituents, drink with them, lodge with them, pray with them, laugh, hunt, dance and work with them; I eat their corn dodgers and fried bacon, and sleep two in a bed with them. Among my first acquaintances were the L——s, down under the Bluffs. Fine fellows, the L——s,—by the way, I am sure of five votes there. Well, you perceive, I had to live there: and I did live there. But, sir, I was frightened the first night I slept there. I own it; yes, sir, I acknowledge the corn. An ice in August is something: but I was done to an icicle; had periodical chills for ten days. Did you ever see a Venus in linsey-woolsey?"

"No!"

"Then you shall see Serena L——s. They call her the 'White Plover:' seventeen:—plump as a pigeon, and smooth as a persimmon. How the devil, said I to myself, soliloquizing the first night I slept there, am I to go to bed before this young lady? I do believe my heart was topsyturvied, for the idea of pulling off my boots before the girl was death. And as to doffing my other fixtures, I would sooner have my leg taken off with a wood-saw. The crisis was tremendous. It was nearly midnight, and the family had been hours in bed. Miss Serena alone remained. Bright as the sun, the merry minx talked on. It was portentously obvious to me at last, that she had determined to outsit me. By repeated spasmodic efforts, my coat, waistcoat, cravat, boots and socks were brought off. During the process, my beautiful neighbour talked to me with unaverted eyes, and with that peculiar kind of placidity employed by painters to imbody their idea of the virgin. I dumped myself down in a chair, in a cold perspiration. A distressing thought occurred to me. Does not the damsel stand on a point of local etiquette? It may be the fashion of these people to see strangers in bed before retiring themselves? May I not have kept those beautiful eyes open, from ignorance of what these people deem good breeding? Neither the lady's eyes nor tongue had indeed betrayed fatigue. Those large jet eyes seemed to dilate and grow brighter as the blaze of the wood fire died away; but doubtless this was from kind consideration for the strange wakefulness of her guest. The thing was clear. I determined to retire, and without delay. I arose with firmness, unloosed my suspenders, and in a voice not altogether steady, said:

"'Miss Serena, I think I will retire.'

"'Certainly, sir,' she quietly observed, 'you will lodge there, sir;' inclining her beautiful head towards a bed standing a few yards from where she was sitting. I proceeded to uncase; entrenching myself behind a chair the while, fondly imagining the position offered some security. It is simply plain to a man in his senses, that a chair of the fashion of the one I had thrown between myself and 'the enemy,' as a military man would say, offered almost no security at all. No more, in fact, than standing up behind a ladder—nothing in the way of the artillery of bright eyes, as a poet would say, sweeping one down by platoons. Then I had a dead open space of ten feet between me and the bed; a sort of Bridge of Lodi passage which I was forced to make, exposed to a cruel raking fire fore and aft. Although I say it, who should not say it, an emergency never arose for which I had not a resource. I had one for this. The plan was the work of a moment, I de——"

"Ah! I see, you stormed the battery and s——"

"Bah! don't interrupt me. No; I determined, by a bold ruse de guerre, to throw her attention out of the window, clear the perilous passage, and fortify myself under the counterpane before she recovered her surprise. The plan failed. You see I am a small man, physically speaking. Body, limbs, and head, setting up business on one hundred and seven and a half pounds, all told, of flesh, blood, and bones, cannot, individually or collectively, set up any very ostentatious pretensions. I believe the young lady must have been settling in her mind some philosophical point on that head. Perhaps her sense of justice wished to assure itself of a perfectly fair distribution of the respective motives. Perhaps she did not feel easy until she knew that a kind Providence had not added to general poverty individual wrong. Certain it was, she seemed rather pleased with her speculations; for when I arose from a stooping posture finally, wholly disencumbered of cloth, I noticed mischievous shadows playing about the corners of her mouth. It was the moment I had determined to direct her eye to some astonishing circumstance out of the window. But the young lady spoke at the critical moment.

"'Mr. Douglass,' she observed, 'you have got a mighty small chance of legs there.'

"Men seldom have any notice of their own powers;

I never made any pretensions to skill in ground and lofty tumbling; but it is strictly true, I cleared, at one bound, the open space, planted myself on the centre of the bed, and was buried in the blankets in a twinkling."

"I congratulate you, my boy," said I, poising a cube of the crimson core of the melon on the point of my knife; "a lucky escape truly! But was the young lady modest?"

"Modest, sir!—there is not in Illinois a more modest, or more sensible girl. It's habit—all habit. I think nothing of it now. Why, it's only last week I was at a fine wedding party, and a large and fine assembly of both sexes lodged in the same room, with only three feet or so of neutral territory between them."

"You astonish me, Mr. Douglass."

"Fact, sir, upon my honour. You see these people are the very soul of hospitality, and never allow a fine social party to turn out at twelve o'clock at night to go long distances home. All that is more cleverly managed here. An Illinois bed has a power of elongation or expansion perfectly enigmatical to strangers. One bed four feet wide, will, on occasion, flank one whole side of the house, and is called a field-bed, and large parties will range themselves on opposite sides of the house as economically as candles in a box."

"But, my dear fellow, this is drouthy prose, introduce yourself to that little fellow in the corner, and pass him over; and now tell me all about old Canandaigua."

This story of Judge Douglass has suggested to Field, of the St. Louis "Reveille," the following adventure of a Missouri politician:—

The "gentleman of Illinois" is not the only gentleman whose *legs* have led him into embarrassment. A political friend of ours, equally happy in his manners, if not in his party, among the Missouri constituency, found himself, while canvassing the State, last summer, for Congress, in even a *more* peculiarly perplexing predicament than the Illinois judge.

There is a spot in the south-western part of this State, known as *The Fiery Fork of Honey Run!*—a delicious locality, no doubt, as the *run* of "honey" is of course accompanied by a corresponding flow of "milk," and a mixture of milk and honey, or at any rate, honey and "peach," is the evidence of sublunary contentment, every place where they have preaching!

"Honey Run," further Christianized by the presence of an extremely hospitable family whose mansion, comprising *one apartment*—neither more nor less—is renowned for being never shut against the traveller, and so our friend found it during the chill morning air, at the expense of a rheumatism in his shoulder, its numerous unaffected cracks and spaces clearly showing, that dropping the latch was a useless formality. The venerable host and hostess, in their one apartment, usually enjoy the society of two sons, four daughters, sundry dogs and "niggers," and as many lodgers as may deem it prudent to risk the somewhat equivocal allotment of sleeping partners. On the night in question, our friend, after a hearty supper of ham and eggs, and a canvass of the *Fiery Forkers*, the old lady having pointed out his bed, felt very weary, and only looked for an opportunity to "turn in," though the mosquitoes were trumping all sorts of wrath, and no net appeared to *bar* them. The dogs flung themselves along the floor, or again rose, restlessly, and sought the door-step; the "niggers" stuck their feet in the yet warm ashes; the old man stripped, unscrupulously, and sought his share of the one collapsed-looking pillow, and the sons, cavalierly followed his example, leaving the old woman, "gals," and "stranger," to settle any question of delicacy that might arise.

The candidate yawned, looked at his bed, went to the door, looked at the daughters; finally, in downright recklessness, seating himself upon "the downy," and pulling off his coat. Well, he *pulled* off his coat—and he folded his coat—and then he yawned—and then he whistled—and then he called the old lady's attention to the fact, that it would *never* do to sleep in his muddy trousers—and then he *undid* his vest—and then he whistled again—and then, suddenly, an idea of her lodger's possible embarrassment seemed to flash upon the old woman, and she cried—

"*Gals*, jest turn your backs round 'till the *stranger* gits into bed."

The backs were turned, and the stranger *did* get into bed in "less than no time," when the hostess again spoke.

"Reckon, stranger, as you aint used to us, you'd better *kiver up* till the *gals* undress, hadn't you?"

By this time our friend's sleepy fit was over, and though he did "kiver up," as desired, somehow or other, the old counterpane was equally kind in hiding his blushes, and favouring his sly glances. The nymphs were soon stowed away, for there were neither bustles to unhitch nor corsets to unlace, when their mamma, evidently anxious not to smother her guest, considerately relieved him.

"You can un*kiver* now, stranger; I'm *married folks*, and you aint afeared o' *me*, I reckon!"

The stranger happened to be "married folks," himself; he un*kivered*, and turned his back with true connubial indifference, as far as the ancient lady was concerned, but, with regard to the "gals," he declares that his half-raised curiosity inspired the most tormenting dreams of *mermaids* that ever he experienced.

A MILLERITE MIRACLE.

BY C. A. P., OF KENTUCKY.

In the following sketch is displayed in bold relief the mummeries practised by Miller, Himes, and others, who have followed in the footsteps of Matthias "the prophet," and humbugs of like stamp. It is from the pen of a new correspondent of the "Spirit of the Times."

In a little village in the state of Hoosierana, in the year 1844, there was "all sorts" of excitement concerning the doctrines and prophesies of that arch-deceiver, Miller. For months the Midnight Cry, followed by the Morning Howl, and the Noonday Yell, had circulated through the village and surrounding counties, to an extent not even equalled by Dr. D.'s celebrated speech. Men disposed of their property for little or nothing. The women were pale and ghastly from watching and praying, and in fact, the whole population, or at least those who believed in the coming ascension, looked as if they were about half-over a second attack of the chills and fever. There were, however, some "choice spirits," (not choice in theirs, however,) who, notwithstanding the popularity of the delusion, would not enlist under the banners of the ascensionists, and among these was a wild, harumscarum blade from "Down East," by the name of Cabe Newham. Now Cabe was as hard "a case" as you would meet on a fourth of July in Texas, always alive for fun and sport of any and every description, and a strong disbeliever in Millerism.

The night of the third of April was the time agreed upon out west here, for the grand exhibition of "ground and lofty tumbling," and about ten o'clock of the said night, numbers of the Millerites assembled on the outskirts of the town, on a little eminence, upon which the proprietor had allowed a few trees to stand. In the crowd, and the only representative of his race present, was a free negro by the name of Sam, about as ugly, black, woolly, and rough a descendant of Ham as ever baked his shins over a kitchen fire.

Sam's head was small, body and arms very long, and his legs bore a remarkable resemblance to a pair of hames; in fact, put Sam on a horse, his legs clasped round its neck, his head towards the tail, and his arms clasped round the animal's hams, and at ten paces off you would swear he was an *old set of patent gearing.*

The leader of the Millerites, owing to an "ancient grudge he bore him," hated Sam "like smoke," and had done all in his power to prevent his admittance among the "elect," but all to no purpose; Sam would creep in at every meeting, and to-night here he was again, dressed in a white robe of cheap cotton, secured to his body by a belt, and shouting and praying as loud as the best.

Now on the morning of the third, Cabe had, with a deal of perseverance, and more trouble, managed to throw a half-inch hemp cord over the branch of an oak, which stretched its long arm directly over the spot where the Millerites would assemble; one end he had secured to the body of the tree, and the other to a stump some distance off. About ten o'clock, when the excitement was getting about "eighty pounds to the inch," Cabe, wrapped in an old sheet, walked into the crowd, and proceeded to fasten, in as secure a manner as possible, the end of the rope to the back part of the belt which confined Sam's robe, and having succeeded, "sloped" to join some of his companions who had the other end. The few stars in the sky threw a dim light over the scene, and in a few moments the voice of Sam was heard, exclaiming "Gor Almighty! I'se a goin' up! Who-o-oh!" and sure enough, Sam was seen mounting into the "ethereal blue;" this was, however, checked when he had cleared "terra firma" a few feet. "Glory!" cried one, "Hallelujah!" another, and shrieks and yells made night hideous; some fainted, others prayed, and not a few dropped their robes and "slid." Now, whether it was owing to the lightness of his head, or the length and weight of his heels, or both, Sam's position was not a pleasant one; the belt to which Cabe's cord was attached was bound exactly round his centre of gravity, and Sam swung like a pair of scales, head up and heels down, heels up and head down, at the same time sweeping over the crowd like a pendulum, which motion was accelerated by his strenuous clapping of hands and vigorous kicking. At length he became alarmed, he *wouldn't* go up, and he couldn't come down! "Lor a massy," cried he, "jist take up poor nigger to um bosom, or lef him down again, *easy*, *easy*. Lef him down again, please um Lor, and dis nigger will go straight to um bed! Ugh-h-h," and Sam's teeth chattered with affright, and he kicked again more vigorously than before, bringing his head directly downward and his heels up, when a woman shrieking out, "Oh! Brother Sam, take me with you," sprung at his head as he swept by her, and caught him by the wool, bringing him up "all standing." "Gosh! Sister," cried Sam, "lef go um poor nigger's *har.*" Cabe gave another pull at the rope, but the additional weight was too much, the belt gave way and down came Sam, his bullet head taking the leader of the saints a "feeler" just between the eyes. "Gosh, is I down agin?" cried the bewildered Sam, gathering himself up. "I is, bress de Lor! but I was nearly dar, I seed de gate!" The leader wiped his overflowing proboscis, took Sam by the nape of the neck, led him to the edge of the crowd, and giving him a kick, said, "Leave, you cussed baboon! you are so ugly *I know'd they wouldn't let you in.*"

OLD SINGLETIRE,

THE MAN THAT WAS NOT ANNEXED.

BY THE LATE ROBERT PATTERSON, ESQ., OF LOUISIANA.

The writer of the following incident was a long time associated with the author of "Tom Owen, the Bee Hunter"—T. B. Thorpe, Esq.—in editing the "Concordia Intelligencer." He was a remarkably clever man, and his early death last season has deprived his contemporaries of a most entertaining and worthy member of the "press gang."

A GOOD story is told of this bold frontiersman, who had made himself notorious, and given his character the *bend sinister*, by frequent depredations on both sides the boundary line between Texas and the United States. The old fellow had migrated thither from parts unknown, years since, knew every foot of country for fifty miles on either side in his vicinity, and had communication by runners with many "*birds of the same feather*," then common in the region.

The old fellow saw, with sorrow and regret, the rapid influx of population within the last ten years, and was compelled gradually to narrow his sphere of *usefulness*, for, said he, "People's a gittin too thick about me—tha and their varmints and critters is fillin up the woods and spilin the huntin—and then tha aint no chance for a fellar to *speculate* upon travellers as tha used to be when tha wan't any body to watch a fellar :—why, tha is get-en to be so *civylizated* that a fellar can't drink a barrel of double-rectified 'thout havin' em all abusin' him about it—and then ef he doas happen jist by accident to drap half an ounce of lead into a feller, why tha is all up in arms about it. Now t'other day when I wanted to mark Joe Sliteses' ears like tha marks their hogs, 'case he called me a vill-*yan*, they wanted to *jewdicate* me afore the court. But cuse 'em for a set of blasted fools they aint a gwoin to fool 'Old Singletire' ef he is a gitten old and ain't as quick on the trigger as he used to was.

"Blast their skins, I don't care ef tha *does* annexate Texas! I'll show 'em somethin—tho' tha thinks tha is got me slick when tha git the two countries wedged up into one—but I'll fix em, I'll quit and go to ARKANSAW —whar a decent white man kin live 'thout bein' pestered, and bused and *jewdicated!*"

"Old Single" as he was called, *for short*, had several years previous to the late discussion of the annexation question, with singular 'cuteness ascertained the precise line dividing the two territories, and built his cabin thereon in such a position that when lying down—*he slept, one half in the United States, and the other half in Texas*, for he lay at right angles with the line.

The authorities of both sides had frequently found him in that position, but as their separate claims lay severally on the *entire* individual, they were not content to arrest *one half of him* at a time. A great deal of courtesy was at times exhibited by the officers, each pressing the other to break the forms of international law by pulling Old Single bodily over either side the line. Each was up to trap, and feared the other wished to trick him, and declined the effort which might cause a rupture between Texas and the Union.

On one occasion they were exceedingly pressing on the subject, at first politely so, then teasing each other, and then daring by taunt, and jeer, and jibe, until they worked themselves into such furious excitement that "Old Single," their pretended victim, had to command and preserve the peace—"Gentle-*men*," said he, "you may fun, and fret, and quarrel jist as much as you please in my house—but when tha is any lickin to be done 'bout these diggins, why 'Old Single' is *thar sure!*—so look out boys, ef you strikes you *dies*: —show your sense, make friends, and let's *liker.* You," nodding to one, "hand me a gourd of water; and, You," to another, "pass that bottle and I'll drink to your better 'quaintance."

The day passed, "Old Single" crosses the line, and one of the *beauties* on each side his cot, all going it like forty at twenty-deck poker—a sociable game as Sol. Smith says—and as remarked our informant, "the old man was a perfect *Cumanche horse* at any game whar tha was *curds.*"

For the last three months "Old Single" had been mightily distressed—"*mighty oneasy bout annexation*" —for he knew he would be compelled to travel—well the news of the action of Texas on this great question was received in "Old Single's" vicinity on 29th of June—the day it reached Fort Jessup.

Next morning "the boys" from Boston and De Kalb, a couple of border villages—after a glory gathering about annexation, determined to storm "Old Single" and "*rout*" him. They accordingly, *en masse a-la-*

regulator, started off for his cabin, and on arriving near it, a consultation was held, and it was determined that bloodshed was useless—as it was certain to occur if violence was resorted to—and that a flag of truce should be sent into the fortress, offering terms.

The old man was found in a gloomy mood, with a pack strapped to his back, in woodsman style. "Old *Centresplit*, his friend of thirty years' standing, his rifle, his favourite—his all—was laid across his knees, and he in deep thought, his eyes resting on vacancy. As the delegation entered, he looked up, "Well, boys, the time is *cum*, and Texas and you is annixated, *but I aint*, and I *aint a gwoin to be nuther!—so take care how you raise my dander; I can shoot sum yet!*"

The party explained, and it was agreed the old fellow should take up the march *upon the line* for the nearest point on Red River, the party escorting him at twenty paces distant on either side—that the last mile should be run—that if he struck the water's edge first, he should go free—if otherwise, he was to be taken and rendered up a victim to the offended dignity of the laws. "*Agreed*," said Old Single, "it's a bargain. Boys, tha is a *gallon* in that barrel, let's finish it in a friendly way, and then travel." The thing was done, the travel accomplished, and the race, fast and furious, was being done. The old fellow led the crowd, hallooing at his topmost voice as he gained the river—"HOOPEE!—HURRAH!—*I aint annixated!—I'm off—I aint no whar—nuther in the States nor Texas*, BUT IN ARKANSAW!!!" swam to the opposite shore, fired a volley, gave three cheers, and retired victorious.

"RUNNING A SAW" ON A FRENCH GENTLEMAN.

BY "GINSANGANDSON," OF PHILADELPHIA.

One of the most amusing correspondents of the "Spirit of the Times" is "the gentleman with the hard name," whose *nomme de plume* is quoted above. In more respects than we care to state, he is, emphatically, "a host in himself," as every Philadelphian, and the travelling community generally, will bear willing testimony.

A Frenchman who had been residing some years in London, and appeared to be very vain of his knowledge of mankind, was detailing to some of his compatriots in this country a little adventure which happened to him in The Great Metropolis. I give you the story in his own words as much as possible, his manner you must conceive.

"When I was in Londres, I go vun day into wat ze Anglais call ze café, an I give ze order to ros me von docke; ze Anglais ros ze docke ver well; ven de docke was place before me I find him von ver fine docke, and ver well ros; he was ver brown, ver full of ze stuff aux ognons, an ze flaveur was ver fine. I put ze fork into ze docke and I commence to cut ze docke, mais when I have begin to cut ze docke I hear some person make loud strong noise comme ça—Oh——! as if ze heart was break. I put down ze knife on ze plate, an I look roun to see who make ze noise comme ça—Oh——! Ven I look roun I see right opposite to me von gentlman, who was ver well dress; he ave ver good cote, ver good pantalon, and ver good boot, but he have dam leetle hat wiz a hole in ze top; *I no like dat*, mais he was a gentlman; ze noise could not be made by him, an I proceed to cut ze docke, mais, ver I ave proceed to cut ze docke ze second time, I hear une autre fois ze same noise, comme ça—Oh——! plus forte, grate deal loudaire zan ze first time. I look roun, mais I see nobody but ze gentlman; I look at ze gentlman, an ze gentlman look at me. He *vas* gentlman, for he ave ver good cote, ver good pantalon, and ver good boot, mais he ave dam leetle hat on ze head wiz a hole in ze top, an ze hair come out; *I no like dat*, mais he *vas* gentlman. Eh bien! I ave say to ze gentlman—'Monsieur, pour quoi you make comme ça—Oh——!?' and ze gentlman ave make me answer an say, 'Sare, I ave eat nosing for tree day, an I am ver hungry.' Mon dieu, I say to myself, ze gentlman ave reason, he ave eat nosing for tree day. Sacre-bleu he must ave ver grate hungaire, an ven I ave say dis to myself I look at ze docke, he was ver fine docke, an ver well ros. Zen I say to myself ze seconde time, I shall give ze half of ze docke to ze gentlman, an zen I give ze invitation to ze gentlman, to partage ze docke wiz me. Ven ze gentlman ave receive ze invitation he rite way place himself vis a vis to me, an ma fois! ausi quick as ze lightnin he ave eat *ze hole of my docke, Bigod*, quel faim! Ze gentlman ave speak ze truf, he was ver hungry! En verité, I should like to eat piece of my docke, mais ven I zink ze gentlman ave eat nosing for tree day, an as for me I ave dejuner tres forte, I ring ze bell an I give ze order for a noser docke; in ze mean time, however, ze gentlman ave drink ze hole of my wine. Eh bien, I I deman ze oder bouteille, an zen ze oder docke come; ver fine docke, mais not so good as ze last,—n'importe, ze docke was ver good, mais dis time I ave cut ze docke for me, an ze gentlman ave got ze oser piece, he was so hungry, quel dammage, so mooch a gentlman, so well he dress. He ave ver good cote, ver good pantalon, an ver good boot, mais ze dam leetle hat wiz ze hole in ze top; *I no like dat*, but he WAS gentlman. Eh bien, apres ça ze gentlman was satisfy he ave eat nearly ze two docke, an I was satisfy, an ven I ave settle ze conte ze lanlor was satisfy aussi; an zen I ave say to ze gentlman, 'Monsieur, I sall ave ze plaisir to see you some oser time, demain chez vous, at your house,' and ze gentlman he make grate noise, un autre fois for ze zurd time, comme ça—Oh——! an he say to me, 'Sare, I ave no house.' Eh bien! I reply to him, vare do you slip? an he say to me, 'Sare, I slip in ze street.' Bigod, I say to myself, wat grate pitie such hansome gentlman slip in ze street; an zen I look at him again, an I know he is gentlman, he ave such ver good cote, such ver good pantalon, an such ver good boot, but zen I see ze *dam* leetle hat wiz ze hole in ze top, *I no like dat!* but he was gentlman. Nevare min, I shall take ze gentlman chez moi to my house! bigod he shall not slip in ze street! So I give him ze invitation to go to my house, which he ave accept with great plaisir. Ven I ave take him chez moi I make in ze corner what ze Anglais call ze shake-down,—shake-up! an ze gentlman commence already to take off ze close. Pour la premiere he ave put ze dam leetle hat wiz ze hole in ze top on ze chair, *I no like*, so when he ave turn his back, I give it von leetle kick under ze bed and nevare say nosing; ze gentlman zen take off ze cote, ver good cote—ver good cote indeed! an he take off ze pantalon, ver fine pantalon, ver good pantalon—oui, ver good! an zen he take off ze boot, ah ma fois, zey were good boot, ver fine boot indeed, an ze gentlman he go to slip. Eh bien, c'est fine, I ave nosing else to do, I go to slip aussi, an I nevaire hear nosing at all tout la nuit, I mus have slip ver well. In ze morning, ver early, à la bonne heur, I rub my eyes an fine myself wake up; I put ze head out of ze bed an I look for my compagnon, mais ze gentlman I no see him, no doute he slip ver mooch hard, he have grand fatigue he slip all ze time in ze street, I ave grate compassion for him; so I turn on ze oser side an I make ze second time wat ze Anglais call ze leetle nappe, not ze 'nappe Francaise,' mais ze 'nappe Anglaise;' chose tres difference je vous assuré. Eh bien, ven I ave rub ze eye ze second time, I fin it was ten o'clock of ze watch, an I say to ze gentleman who have slip in ze corner all ze nite, 'Monsieur, levez vous! it is time to get up,' an ze gentlman ave make no response, an zin I get up myself an I look in ze corner, mais I fin nosing, ze gentlman was gone. Ah ha! I say to myself, ze gentlman was tres reconnaisant, he ave ver mooch gratitude, he mus ave wake up an he fin me slip ver good, he no like to make ze noise to disturb me; I ave no dout he will come back ven he zink I ave wake up, an he will make me grate zank for my kindness to him zat he did not slip in ze street. Oh he is such gentlman, he ave such ver good cote, such fine pantalon, and such ver good boot. Ven I say zis to myself I zink make my toillette, an I put on my boot, ver good boot,—mais, wat it is—*zey are not my boot!* ver good boot indeed—*ver* good boot! mais zey are *not my* boot. Ah nevaire min, it is mistake, ze gentlman ave made mistake, he get up so early in ze morning an ave make ze mistake in ze dark. Eh bien, he will soon return and make ze grand apologie, for he is so mooch gentlman—oh oui, he is gentlman, he ave ver good cote, ver good pantalon, an ze boot are ver good aussi—not so good as mine, mais ze are ver good. In ze mean time I zink comme ça to myself, an I look roun for my pantalon; oh zey are zere. I put on ze pantalon, mais—que diable! I feel in ze poches, oui, bigar zey are not *my pantalon—ver fine!* oui, ver fine pantalon, mais zey are not my pantalon. Ah tis ver plain, ze gentlman ave make anoser mistake, an ave take my pantalon, an zink zey are his pantalon; nevaire min! nevaire min! he will fine out ze mistake bomby when he fine ze monnaie in ze poche, he will be ver sorry, for he is gentlman, he ave such ver good cote, ver good pantalon, an ver good boot; oh oui, he is gentlman, j'en suis sure. Vile I zink so to myself I look at ze watch, an I fine him leven o'clock of ze mornin; I tink it is time to break ze faste, I am ver hungry, so I put on my—ze debil! what I have here?—ver fine coat, mais, ouis, it is not my cote—no it is *not my cote!* Bigod ze gentlman ave make un autre fois, a noser gran mistake, he ave take my cote an lef me his cote, it was ver good cote—ver good cote indeed! mais it was not my cote.

"Wat ze debbil I got here! *Ze dam leetle hat wiz ze hole in ze top;* bigar! *I no like dat."—Page* 73.

J'en suis faché ven ze gentlman ave fine it out he will be mooch mortify zat he ave take my cote. Ah mon Dieu! I ave grate pitie for him, he was such gentlman, I am sure he was gentlman, he ave such *ver* good cote, such fine pantalon, and such ver good boot! Oh certainement he was gentlmen, I nevaire make ze mistake, I know ze gentlman an he was gentlman, I know he will come back; an zen I wait for him von hour by ze clock, an I zink to myself, bigar I ave ze gran rumble in ze stomac, an I feel ver hungere as if I ave eat nosing for tree day like ze gentlman, who I ave no doubt ave wait all zis time at ze café for me. Ah quel shepide! I nevaire zink of zat before, an I look for my hat. It is not on ze table,—no! it is not on ze——restez! q'avons nous ici? Who put my hat under ze bed? my new hat! I ave jus buy him, an ave jus pay von guinea for him; Venez! I go on ze knee. Ah ha! I ave got him by ze ear. *Venez ici donc, rodeur!—Bigod! wat ze debil I got here! Hein? Sacre-bleu! mille tonnerres! ze dam leetle hat wiz ze hole in ze top, bigar! I no like dat*, ze gentlman ave make von dam gran mistake dis time, *an I no like dat.* Mais he *was* gentlman, he ave such ver good cote, such ver fine pantalon, and such good boot, mais I no like ze dam leetle hat *wiz ze hole in ze top.*— No! Bigod!! Mais he was gentlman."

BREAKING A BANK.

BY SOL. SMITH, AUTHOR OF "THEATRICAL APPRENTICESHIP AND ANECDOTAL RECOLLECTIONS.'

We cannot allow a second collection of stories from the "Spirit of the Times" to go before the public without containing one of Sol. Smith's sketches, he having been one of our earliest correspondents. Besides which, it is not contained in the Appendix to his own admirable collection of stories, recently published in Philadelphia.

Captain Summons is a very clever fellow—and the "Dr. Franklin" *was* a very superb boat, albeit inclined to rock about a good deal, and nearly turn over on her side when visited by a breath of air in the least resembling a gale. Capt. Summons is a clever fellow. All steamboat captains are clever fellows—or *nearly* all; but what I mean to say is, Captain Summons is a *particularly* clever fellow!—a clever fellow in the widest sense of the term—a fellow that is clever in every way—anxious that his passengers shall be comfortably bestowed, well fed and well attended to—and *determined* that they shall amuse themselves "just as they d—n please," as the saying is. If he happens to have preachers on board, he puts on a serious countenance of a Sunday morning—consents that there shall be preaching—orders the chairs to be set out, and provides Bibles and hymn-books for the occasion—himself and officers, whose watch is below, taking front seats and listening attentively to the discourse. Likely as not, at the close of the service, he will ask the reverend gentleman who has been officiating, with his back in close proximity to a hot fire in a Franklin furnace, to accompany him to the bar and join him in some refreshments! If there are passengers on board who prefer to pass the time away in playing poker, ucre, brag, or whist, tables and chairs are ready for *them*, too—poker, brag, ucre and whist be it! All sorts of passengers are accommodated on the Dr. Franklin—the rights of none are suffered to be infringed;—all are free to follow such employments as shall please themselves. A *dance* in the evening is a very common occurrence on this boat, and when cotillions are *on the carpet*, the captain is sure to be *thar*.

It sometimes happens that, at the commencement of a voyage, it is found somewhat difficult to reconcile *all* the passengers to the system of Capt. Summons, which is founded on the broad principle of equal rights to all. On the occasion of my voyage in the "Doctor," in December, 1844, I found myself surrounded by a crowd of passengers who were *entire strangers* to me—a very rare occurrence to one who travels so often on the western rivers as I do. I wished my absence from New Orleans to be as brief as possible, and the "Doctor" was the fastest boat in port at the time of my leaving the Crescent City; so I resolved to secure a berth in her, and trust in luck to find a St. Louis boat at the Mouth.

I don't know how it is, or *why* it is, but by strangers I am almost always taken for a PREACHER. It was so on this voyage. There were three Methodist *circuit* riders on board; and it happened that we got acquainted, and were a good deal together—from which circumstance I was supposed to be *one of them;* which supposition was the means of bringing me into an acquaintance with the lady passengers, who, for the most part, were very pious, religiously inclined souls. We had preaching every day, and sometimes at night; and I must say, in justice to brothers Twitchel and Switchell, that their sermons were highly edifying and instructive.

In the mean time, a portion of the passengers "at the other end of the hall" continued to play sundry games with cards, notwithstanding the remonstrances of the worthy followers of Wesley, who frequently requested the captain to interfere and break up such unholy doings. The captain had but one answer—it was something like this: "Gentlemen, amuse yourselves as you like; preach and pray to your hearts' content—none shall interfere with your pious purposes; some like that sort of thing—*I* have no objection to it. These men prefer to amuse themselves with cards; let them—they pay their passage as well as you, gentle*men,* and have as much right to *their* amuse*ments* as you have to *yours,* and they shall not be disturbed. Preach, play cards, dance cotillions—do what you like, *I* am agreeable; only understand that *all games* (preaching among the rest) *must cease at ten o'clock.*" So *we* preachers got very little comfort from Captain Summons.

Up—up, up—up we went. Christmas day arrived. All the *other* preachers had holden forth on divers occasions, and it being ascertained that it was my intention to leave the boat on her arrival at Cairo, a formal request was preferred, that *I should preach the Christmas sermon!* The LADIES (God bless them all!) were *very* urgent in their applications to me. "Oh *do*, brother Smith! we *want* to hear *you* preach! All the others have contributed their share to our spiritual comfort—you *must* oblige us—indeed you must." I endeavoured to excuse myself the best way I could, alleging the necessity of my leaving the boat in less than an hour—my baggage was not ready—I had a terrible cold, and many other good and substantial reasons were given; but all in vain—preach I must. "Well," thinks I, "if I must, I must." At this crisis, casting my eyes down towards the Social Hall, and seeing an unusual crowd assembled around a table, I asked one of the brethren what might be going on down there? The fattest of the preaching gentlemen replied—"The poor miserable sinners have filled the measure of their iniquity by opening a FARO BANK!" "Horrible!" exclaimed I, holding up my hands—and "horrible!" echoed the ladies and missionaries in full chorus. "Cannot such doings be put a stop to?" asked an elderly lady, addressing the pious travellers. "I fear not," groaned my Methodist contemporary, (the fat one.) "We have been trying to convince the captain that some dreadful accident will inevitably befall the boat, if such proceedings are permitted—and what do you think he answered?" "What?" we all asked, of course. "Why, he just said, that, inasmuch as he permitted *us* to preach and pray, he should let other passengers dance and play, if they chose to do so; and that, if I didn't like the 'proceedings' I complained of *I might leave the boat!* Yes—he did; and, moreover, he mentioned that it was eleven o'clock, and asked me if I wouldn't 'liquor!'" This announcement of the captain's stubbornness and impiety was met with a general groan of pity and sorrow, and we resumed the conversation respecting the unhallowed faro bank. "It is much to be regretted," remarked the elderly lady who had spoken before, "that *something* can't be done—Brother Smith," she continued, appealing directly to me, and laying her forefinger impressively upon my arm, "cannot *you* break up that bank?" "Dear Madam," I answered, "you know not the difficulty of the task you impose upon me—FARO BANKS ARE NOT SO EASILY BROKEN UP as you may imagine; however, as you all appear so anxious about it, if you'll excuse me from the sermon, I'll see what can be done." "Ah! that's a dear soul!"—"I knew he would try"—"He'll be sure to succeed!"—"Our prayers shall not be wanting!" Such were the exclamations that greeted me, as I moved off towards the faro bank. Elbowing my way into the crowd, I got near the table in front of the dealer, and was for a time completely concealed from the view of my pious friends near the door of the ladies' cabin. I found the bank was a small affair. The betters were risking trifling sums, ranging from six to twenty-five cents.

"Mr. Dealer," I remarked, "I have come to break up this bank." "The deuse you have!" replied the banker—"let's see you do it." "What amount have you in bank?" I inquired. "Eleven dollars," was his answer. "What is your limit?" asked I. "A dollar," he replied. "Very well," said I, placing a ragged Indiana dollar behind the queen—"turn on." He turned, and the king won for me. I took the two dollars up and let him make another turn, when I replaced the bet, and the queen came up in my favour; I had now four dollars, which I placed in the square, taking in the 5, 6, 7, and 8—and it won again! Here were seven dollars of the banker's money. I pocketed three of them, and bet four dollars behind the queen again; the Jack won, and the BANK WAS BROKEN! The crowd dispersed in all directions, laughing at the breaking up of the petty bank, and I made my way towards the ladies' cabin, where my new friends were anxiously awaiting the result of my bold attempt. "Well, well, well," they all exclaimed—"What success?—have you done it? Do let us hear all about it!" I wiped the perspiration from my brow, and putting on a very serious face, I said solemnly: "I HAVE BROKEN THAT BANK!" "You have?" they all exclaimed.—"Yes, I'll be d—d if he hasn't!" muttered the disappointed gamester, the keeper of the late bank, who was just going into his state-room. In the midst of the congratulations which were showered upon me, I received a *summons* from the captain to come forward with my baggage—we were at Cairo.

TAKING THE CENSUS.

Some rich scenes occur in taking the Census under the late law of the State of New York for that purpose. The following, from an eye witness, is one:

"Is the head of the family at home?" asks the inquiring marshal.

"Here's the devil with his book again for the *d'rectry*," shouts a junior of the family to the maternal head above stairs, who presently appears. "Is it the heads of the family ye want sure; but last week ye wanted our name for ye *d'rectry* an' now ye want our *heads?* A free country this, sure, when one's head is not safe. Be off, and bad luck to ye and all like ye." After some explanations, the questions in order are asked.

"Who is the head of the family?"

"Ann Phelim, yer honor, the same in ould Ireland for ever."

"How many Males in this family?"

"Three *males* a day with prateys for dinner an"—

"But how many Men and Boys?"

"Och, why there's the ould man an' the boy and three children who died five years ago, heaven rest their dear souls, the swatest jewils that iver"—

"But how many are now living?"

"Meself, and me daughter Judy, ye see them, and a jewil of a girl she is indeed."

"But have you no males in your family?"

'Sorra the one; the ould man works hard by the day,

and Patrick is not at home at all, but to his males and his bed."

"How many are subject to Military duty?"

"Niver a one; Patrick and the ould man belong to the *Immits*, and sure finer looking soldiers were niver born: did ye not see him when the old Gineral was buried? 'twould have made your heart beat to see two such fine lookin' gintale well-behaved boys."

"How many are entitled to vote?"

"Why the ould man and meself and Judy, and warn't it we that bate the Natives an' the Whigs an' all, an' elicted ould General Jackson over 'im all. Sorra the day when he died and disappointed us all, for a fine man he was."

"How many coloured persons in your family?"

"Nagers, did you name Nagers? Out man, an' don't be insultin' me. Out wid ye, and niver ask for me *senses* agin—don't ask about me *senses*—whither I have nagers in the family? Yer out of yer senses, yer-self, begone and don't bother me."

DICK HARLAN'S TENNESSEE FROLIC.

BY "S ———L," OF TENNESSEE.

We wish we were at liberty to disclose the name and habitation of the writer of the incident annexed, for then we are assured his friends would insist upon his becoming a more regular correspondent of the "Spirit of the Times," in the columns of which he made his *debut*.

You may talk of your bar hunts, Mister Porter, and your deer hunts, and knottin tigers' tails thru the bung-holes of barrels, an cock fitin, and all that, but if a regular bilt frolick in the Nobs of "Old Knox," don't beat 'em all blind for fun, then I'm no judge of fun, that's all! I said *fun*, and I say it agin, from a *kiss* that cracks like a wagin-whip up to a *fite* that rouses up all out-doors—and as to laffin, why they *invented* laffin, and the *last* laff will be hearn at a Nob dance about three in the morning! I'm jest gettin so I can ride arter the motions I made at one at Jo Spraggins's a few days ago.

I'll *try* and tell you who Jo Spraggins is. He's a squire, a school comishoner, overlooker of a mile of Nob road *that leads towards Roody's still-house*—a fiddler, a judge of a hoss, and a hoss himself! He can belt six shillins worth of corn-juice at still-house rates and travel—can out-shute and out-lie any feller from the Smoky Mounting to Noxville, and, if they'll bar one feller in Nox, I'll say to the old Kaintuck Line! (I'm sorter feared of him, for they say that he lied a jackass to death in two hours!)—can make more spinin-wheels, kiss more spinners, thrash more wheat an more men than any one-eyed man I know on. He hates a circuit rider, a nigger, and a shot gun—loves a woman, old sledge, and sin in eny shape. He lives in a log hous about ten yards squar: it has two rooms, one at the bottom an one at the top of the ladder—has all out ove doors fur a yard, and all the South fur its occupants at times. He gives a frolick onst in three weeks in plowin time, and one every Saturday-nite the balance of the year, and only axes a "fip" for a reel, and two "bits" fur what corn-juice you suck; he throws the galls in, and a bed too in the hay, if you git too hot to locomote. The supper is made up by the fellers; every one fetches sumthin; sum a lick of meal, sum a middlin of bacon, sum a hen, sum a possum, sum a punkin, sum a grab of taters, or a pocket full of peas, or dried apples, an sum only fetches a good appetite and a skin chock full of particular devilry, and if thars been a shutin match for beef the day before, why a *leg* finds its way to Jo's sure, without eny help from the balance of the critter. He gives Jim Smith (the store-keeper over Bay's Mounting) *warnin* to fetch a skane of silk fur fiddle strings, and sum "Orleans" for sweetnin, or not to fetch himself; the silk and sugar has never failed to be thar yet. Jo then mounts Punkinslinger bar backed, about three hours afore sun down, and gives all the galls *item*. He does this a lettle of the slickest—jist rides past in a peart rack, singin,

"Oh, I met a frog, with a fiddle on his back,
A axin his way to the fro–l–i–c–k?
Wha-a-he! wha he! wha he! wha ke he-ke-he!"

That's enuf! The galls nows *that* aint a jackass, so

by sun-down they come pourin out of the woods like pissants out of an old log when tother end's afire, jest "as fine as silk" and full of fun, fixed out in all sorts of fancy doins, from the broad-striped homespun to the sunflower calico, with the thunder-and-lightnin ground. As for silk, if one had a silk gown she'd be too smart to wear it to Jo Spraggins's, fur if she did she'd go home in hir petticote-tale *sartin*, for the homespun wud tare it off of hir quicker nor winkin, and if the sunflowers dident help the homespuns, they woudn't do the silk eny good, so you see that silk is never ratlin about your ears at a Nob dance.

The sun had about sot afore I got the things fed an had Barkmill saddled, (you'll larn directly why I call my poney Barkmill,) but an owl couldent have cotch a rat afore I was in site of Jo's with my gall, Jule Sawyers, up behind me. She hugged me mity tite she was "*so feerd of fallin off* that drated poney." She said she didn't mind a fall, but it mought break hir leg an then good bye frolicks—she'd be fit fur nuthin but to nuss brats ollers arterwards. I now hearn the fiddle ting-tong-ding-domb. The yard was full of fellers, and two tall fine-lookin galls was standin in the door, face to face, holdin up the door posts with their backs, laffin, an castin sly looks into the house, an now an then kickin each other with their knees, an then the one kicked wud bow so perlite, and quick at that, and then they'd laff agin an turn red. Jo was a standin in the hous helpin the galls to hold the facins up, an when they'd kick each other he'd wink at the fellers in the yard an grin. Jule, she bounced off just like a bag of wool-rolls, and I hitched my bark-machine up to a saplin that warn't skinned, so he'd git a craw-full of good fresh bark afore mornin. I giv Jule a kiss to sorter molify my natur an put her in heart like, and in we walked. "Hey! hurray!" said the boys; "My gracious!" said the galls, "if here aint Dick an Jule!" jist like we hadent been *rite thar* only last Saturday nite. "Well, I know we'll have reel now!" "Hurraw!—Go it while you'r young!" "Hurraw for the brimstone kiln—every man praise his country!" "Clar the ring!" "*Misses* Spraggins, drive out these dratted tow-headed brats of your'n—give room!" "Who-oo-whoop! whar's the crock of bald-face, and that gourd of honey? Jim Smith, hand over that spoon, an quit a lickin it like "sank in a bean-pot." "You, Jake Snyder, don't holler so!" says the old 'oman—"why you are worse nor a painter." "Holler! why I was jist *whispering* to that gall on the bed—*who-a-whoopee!* now I'm beginning to *holler!* Did you hear *that*, Misses Spraggins, and be darned to your bar legs? You'd make a nice hemp-brake, you would." "Come here, Suse Thompson, and let me pin your dress behind? Your back looks adzactly like a blaze on a white oak!" "My *back* ain't nuffin to you, Mister Smarty!" "Bill Jones, quit a smashin that ar cat's tail!" "Well let hir keep hir tail clar of my ant killers!" "Het Goins, stop tumblin that bed an tie your *sock!*" "Thankee, marm, its a longer stockin than you've got—*look at it!*" "Jim Clark has gone to the woods for fat pine, and Peggy Willet is along to take a lite for him—they've been gone a coon's age. Oh, here comes the lost 'babes in the wood,' and *no lite!*" "Whar's that lite! whar's that torch! I say, Peggy, whar *is* that bundle of lite wood?" "Why, I fell over a log an lost it, and we hunted clar to the foot of the holler for it, and never found it. It's no account, no how—nuthin but a little pine—who cares?" "Hello, thar, gin us 'Forked Deer," old fiddle-teazer, or I'll give you forked litnin! *Ar* you a goin to tum-tum all nite on that pot-gutted old pine box of a fiddle, *say?*" "Give him a soak at the crock and a lick at the patent bee-hive—it'll *ile* his elbows." "Misses Spraggins, you're a hoss! cook on, don't mind me—I dident aim to slap *you;* it was Suze Winters I *wanted* to hit; but you stooped so fair—" "Yes, and it's well for your good looks that you didn't hit to hurt me, old feller!" "Turn over them rashes of bacon, they're a burnin!" "Mind your own business, Bob Proffit, I've cooked for frolicks afore you shed your petticotes—so jist hush an talk to Marth Giffin! See! she is beckonin to you!" "That's a lie, marm! If he comes a near me I'll unjint his dratted neck! No sech fool that when a gall puts hir arm round his neck will break and run, shall look at *me*, that's flat! Go an try Bet Holden!" "Thankee, marm, I don't take your leavins," says Bet, hir face lookin like a full cross between a gridiron and a steel-trap.

"Whoop! hurraw! Gether your galls for a break down! Give us 'Forked Deer!'" "No, give us 'Natchez-under-the-hill!'" "Oh, Shucks! give us 'Rocky Mounting,' or 'Misses McCloud!'" "'Misses McCloud' be darned, and 'Rocky Mounting' too! jist give us

"She woudent, and she coudent, and she dident come at all!"

"Thar! that's it! Now make a brake! *Tang!* Thar is a brake—a string's gone!" "Thar'll be a head broke afore long!" "Giv him goss—no giv him a horn and every time he stops repeat the dose, and nar another string 'ill brake to nite. Tink-tong! all rite! Now go it!" and if I know what *goin it* is, we *did* go it.

About midnite, Misses Spraggins sung out "stop that ar dancin and come and get your supper!" It was sot in the yard on a table made of forks stuck in the ground and plank of the stable loft, with sheets for table cloths. We had danced, kissed, and drank ourselves into a perfect thrashin-machine apetite, and the vittals *hid* themselves in a way quite alarmin to tavern-keepers. Jo sung out "Nives is scase, so give what thar is to the galls an let the balance use thar paws—they was invented afore nives, eney how. Now, Gents, jist walk into the fat of this land. I'm sorter feerd the honey wont last till day break, but the liquor will, *I think*, so you men when you drink your'n, run an kiss the galls fur sweetnin—let them have the honey—it belongs to them, naturaly!"—"Hurraw, my Jo! You know how to do things rite!" "Well, I rayther think I do; I never was rong but onst in my life an then I mistook a camp meetin for a political speechifyin, so I rid up an axed the speaker 'how much Tarrif there was on rot-gut?' and he said 'about here, there *appeared* to be none!' That rayther sot me, as I was right smartly smoked, myself, jist at that time. I had enough liquor plump in me to swim a skunk, so I come agin at him. I axed him 'Who was the bigest fool the Bible told of?' an he said 'Noah for he'd get *tite*?' *I thought*, mind, I only thought he might be a pokin his dead cat at somebody what lives in this holler; I felt my bristles a raisin my jacket-back up like a tent cloth, so I axed him if he'd '*ever seed the Elephant*?' He said no, but he had seen *a grocery walk*, and he expected to see one *rot down* from its *totterin* looks, purty soon!' Thinks I,

Jo, you're beat at your own game ; I sorter felt mean, so I spurr'd and sot old Punkinslinger to cavortin like he was skeered, an I wheeled and twisted out of *that* crowd, an when I *did* git out of site the way I did sail was a caution to turtles and all the other slow varmints."

Well, we danced, and hurrawed without eny thing of *very* perticular interest to happen, till about three o'clock, when the darndest muss was kicked up you ever did see. Jim Smith sot down on the bed alongside of Bet Holden (the steel-trap gall,) and jist fell to huggin of hir bar fashion. She tuck it very kind till she seed Sam Henry a looking on from behind about a dozen galls, *then* she fell to kickin *an* a hollerin, *an* a screetchin like all rath. Sam he come up an told Jim to let Bet go! Jim told him to go to a far off countrie whar they give away brimestone and throw in the fire to burn it. Sam hit him strate atween the eyes, an after a few licks the fitin *started.* Oh hush! It makes my mouth water now to think what a beautiful row we had. One feller from Cady's Cove, nocked a hole in the bottom of a fryin-pan over Dan Turner's head, and left it a hangin round his neck, the handle flyin about like a long que, ane thar it hung till Jabe Thurman cut it off with a cold chissel next day! That was *his share*, fur that nite, sure. Another feller got nocked into a meal-barrel: he was as mealy as an Irish tater and as *hot* as hoss-radish; when he bursted the hoops and cum out he rared a few. Two fellers fit out of the door, down the hill, and into the creek, and thar ended it, in a quiet way, all alone. A perfect mule from Stock Creek hit *me* a wipe with a pair of windin blades: he made kindlin-wood of them, an I lit on him. We had it head-and-tails fur a very long time, all over the house, but the truth must come and shame my kin, he warped me *nice*, so, jist to save his time *I hollered!* The lickin he give me made me sorter oneasy and hostile like; it wakened my wolf wide awake, so I begin to look about for a man I *could* lick and *no mistake!* The little fiddler come a scrougin past, holdin his fiddle up over his head to keep it *in tune*, for the fitin was gettin tolerable brisk. You're the one, thinks I, and I jist grabbed the dough-tray and split it plumb open over his head! *He* rotted down, right thar, and I paddled his 'tother end with one of the pieces!—while I was a molifyin my feelings in that way his gall slip'd up behind me and fetcht'd me a rake with the pot-hooks. Jule Sawyer was *thar*, and jist *anexed to her* rite off, and a mity nice fite it was. Jule carried enuf har from hir hed to make a sifter, and striped and checked her face nice, like a partridge-net hung on a white fence. She hollered fur hir fiddler, but oh, shaw! he coudent do hir a bit of good; he was too buisy a rubbin first his broken head and then his blistered extremities, so when I thought Jule had given her a plenty I pulled hir off and put hir in a good humour by given hir about as many kisses as would cover a barn door.

Well, I thought at last, if I had a drink I'd be *about done*, so I started for the creek; *and* the first thing I saw was more stars with my eyes shut than I ever did with them open. I looked round, and it was the little fiddler's *big brother!* *I knowed what it meant*, so we locked horns without a word, thar all alone, and I do think we fit an hour. At last some fellers hearn the jolts at the house, and they cum and *dug us out*, for we had fit into a hole whar a big pine stump had burnt out, and thar we was, up to our girths a peggin away, face to face, and *no dodgin!*

Well, it is now sixteen days since that fite, and last nite Jule picked gravels out of my knees as big as squirell shot. Luck rayther run agin me that nite, fur I dident lick eny body but the fiddler, and had three fites—but Jule licked her gall, that's some comfort, and I suppose a feller cant *always* win! Arter my fite in the ground we made friends all round, (except the fiddler—he's hot yet,) and danced and liquored at the tail of every Reel till sun up, when them that was sober enuff went home, and them that was *wounded* staid whar they fell. *I* was in the list of wounded, but could have got away if my bark-mill hadn't *ground* off the saplin and gone home without a parting word; so Dick and Jule had to ride "Shanks' mar," and a rite peart *four-leged* nag she is. She was *weak* in *two* of hir legs, but 'tother two—oh, my stars and possum dogs! they make a man swaller tobacker jist to look at 'em, and feel sorter like a June bug was crawlin up his trowses and the waistband too tite for it to git out. I'm agoin to marry Jule, I swar I am, and *sich* a cross! Think of a locomotive and a cotton gin! Who! whoopee!

"FALLING OFF A LOG," IN A GAME OF "SEVEN-UP."

BY A VIRGINIAN IN MISSISSIPPI.

"The Turkey Runner" is the signature of a gentleman who has written some of the most graphic and amusing original stories ever published in the "Spirit of the Times." His "Swim for a Deer," "Chunkey's Fight with the Panthers," etc., are among the best sporting sketches in the language. We wish he could be induced to write more frequently.

"Hoss and hoss!"

"Yes; 'hoss and hoss,' and my deal!"

"I'll double the bet, and have the whole bottle or none."

"Let me cut, and I'll stand it."

"'Spose we both take a *little* drink first," said Chunkey.

"No: darned if I do! thar aint enough for us both—if I win I'll drink it, and you must wait till a boat comes, if you die! If you win, I'll wait, if I die!"

Such was the conversation between Jim and Chunkey, as they were sitting across a log on the banks of the Yazoo River, surrounded by a cloud of musquitoes, playing "*seven-up*" for a remaining bottle of whisky, which was not enough for the two, and "wouldn't set one forward" *much*. They were just returning from Bear Creek, in Township 17, Range 1, where they had some hands deadening timber, preparatory to opening a plantation in the Fall. They had sent the negroes to the river to take a steamboat, whilst they, with their furniture, and the remains of a forty-two gallon "red-head," came down Deer Creek in a day out into False Lake, through False Lake into Wasp Lake, and down that to where it empties into the Yazoo, and here on the banks of that river our scene opens.

"Go ahead, then," said Chunkey, "shuffle, deal, and win, if you can, but take out that Jack what's torn!"

I took the Jack out, shuffled, dealt, and at it we went. Chunkey looked mighty scared; his eye was sorter oneasy, and dartin about, and he seemed to be choked, as he kept tryin to swaller somethin—the long beard on his face looked powerful black, or else his face looked powerful white, one or the 'yether. We both played mighty slow and careful. The first hand I made "high, low," and Chunkey "game;" the second hand I made "low, Jack," and Chunkey "high, game."

"Four to three," says I.

"Yes, and my deal," said Chunkey.

He gin 'em the Sunflower "shuffle," and I the Big Greasy "cut," and pushed 'em back. Chunkey dealt em mighty slow, and kept tryin to see my cards, but I laid my hand on 'em as fast as they fell on the log, to prevent him from seein the marks. He turned up the Ace of Clubs. When I looked at my hand, *thar* was the King, Jack, Nine, and Deuce,—I led my King—

"High!" says I.

"Low!" said Chunkey, poppin down the Tray.

"Not edzactly," said I, hawlin in the trick, and

leadin the Deuce, and jist as I done so, I seed Chunkey starin over my shoulder, lookin wilder nor a dyin bar. I never seed a man look so awful in my life. I thought he were gwine to have a fit.

"Ya, ya!" said he, "fallin off the log," cryin "*Snake! snake!!*"

I never took time to look, but made a big he-spring about twenty feet in the cane, the har on my head standin stiff as bristles and ratlin like a raftsman's bones, with the Sky Lake ager, and the bad feelins runnin down to my toes. I reckon you never seed a man so afraid of snakes as I is, and I've been so all my life; I'd rather fight the biggest bar in the swamp with his own weapons, teeth and claws, takin it rough and tumble, dependin on my mind and knowledge of a bar's character, than come in contact with a big rusty highland moccasin or rattlesnake, and that's the reason I never hunts in the summer time. When I lived up on Deer Creek, thar was a perfect cord of all sorts, and I used to wear all summer the thickest kind of cow-hide boots, reachin up to my hips, and I *never* went into the field, 'ceptin on a mule, with a double-barreled gun at that. This, Chunkey knowed; and whenever he seed one he gin me warnin. Chunkey aint afraid of snakes; he'd jist as soon eat of a gourd with a snake, as not, if the snake would help himself and not meddle with his licker.

Well, arter lookin about a spell I couldn't see no snake sign, and I then hollered to Chunkey, but darned a word did he say. It then flashed across my mind that as Chunkey fell on the side of the log whar the licker lay, he *might* sorter taste it, as he were dry enough to be able to swaller a little at a time; so I struck a lick back to the log and looked over, and *thar* he lay, jist curled up like a coon in the sunshine, *and the bottle jist glued to his lips*, and the licker runnin down his throat like a storm! darn him, I hadden't no time to think afore I bounced at him! I struck across his snout, and he nailed my thumb in his jaws, and rostled up a handful of dirt and throwed it in my eyes, and that sot me to gwine, and I throwed the licks into him right and left, and I made the fur fly, *I tell you;* but Chunkey stood it like a man! Darned the word did he say; he wouldn't holler, he was *perfectly game!*

"No, that's a fact! I didn't holler; I didn't have time; while you were working away on that gum knot, I were standin up agin a little dog-wood finishin the licker!"

"How comes it that you never wrung in that part of the story about the knot before?"

"'Cause, I'd done got the licker, and I was satisfied; you thought you'd gin me some mighty big licks, and you was satisfied; and it would have been mean in me to crow over you then: you was out of licker, tobacco, and had your fist all skinned and beat as soft as a bar's foot! Oh no, Jim, I'm reasonable, *I is.*"

"Well, *go along;* if I don't set you to gnawin somethin harder than that knot afore long, then my name aint nothin to me, and I don't car for nobody, that's all."

"All sot," says Chunkey, "let's licker. You wanted to know what '*fallin off a log*,' meant, and I thought I'd show you; but, my honey, I'll jist let you know if you'd a hit *me* any of them licks what you struck 'right and left' into that knot, I'd a gin you a touch of panter fistcuffs—a sort of cross of the scratch on the bite—and a powerful strong game it is, in a close fight. Come, gents, let's licker, and then I can beat any man that wars har, for a mighty nice chunk of a poney, at any game of short cards—

Oh, the wagoner was a mighty man, a mighty man was he:
He'd pop his whip, and stretch his chains, and holler 'wo, gee!' '

THE "WERRY FAST CRAB."

BY A MEMBER OF THE "DIGBY CLUB," BOSTON.

Whether "Acorn" or "The Old 'Un"—the editor of the "Morning Post," (who gave these lines "a first rate notice," by the bye,) or "The Young 'Un," was the writer of the following epic—in the style of "Pickle Emmons"—this deponent saith not; he simply commends them to those lovers of horse flesh who are in the habit of sporting their "bits of blood" on the road—a numerous class in which "the b'hoys" greatly predominate.

I.

THEY may talk of their "Fashion,"
And "Bonnets of Blue,"
Of "Blue Dick" and "Ripton,"
And "Confidence" too;
Their owners were lucky,
But I made a grab;
When I bought for a trifle
That "werry fast Crab."

II.

"Chest foundered" and hairless,
And "sprung" though she be,
She's an eye-sore to others,
A good 'un to me;

No market cart, clam cart,
   Or sand cart, or cab,
Can show such a nag
   As my "werry fast Crab."

III.

Braced back in my phaeton,
   A "six" in my jaw,
I touches her up
   On an elegant "raw—"
That I keeps for myself—
   When I gives it a "dab;"
Off flies, like a tortoise,
   My "werry fast Crab."

IV.

Talk of ten miles an hour!
   It causes a smile;
My "werry fast Crab"
   Goes ten hours the mile;
With springs on her fore-knees,
   As slick as a slab,
She stands in her splices,
   My "werry fast Crab."

V.

She's a nice easy keeper,
   I tell you the truth;
And this is the reason,
   She's narry a tooth;
Of the ages of females,
   One ought not to blab,

So I shan't say no more
  Of the age of my "Crab."

VI.

At the next Cambridge races
  Look out for a "splore"—
You'll own you ne'er saw
  Such a critter before:
I'll make at the purse
  A most desperate grab,
If it cost a new "maw"
  On my "werry fast Crab."

"FRENCH WITHOUT A MASTER."

BY "STRAWS," [JOSEPH M. FIELD, ESQ.]

Another "tip-top thing" by the editor of the St. Louis "Reveille," whose sketches of domestic life are among the cleverest of the many which he is in the habit of "throwing off at a heat."

My dear, if that ain't the convenientest book—that French one, with the yaller cover—as ever was; and only to cost twenty-five cents, too! There's Bill and Sally does nothin' else but keep a-askin each other questions in it, and such a jabberin' all round the house, I *never* did see! They can say a good deal more French already than them stuck-up Wilkins' children opposite, that's bin a payin' masters Heaven only knows how long—and here comes the blessed darlin's now, and make 'em go through it before they gets a bit of dinner, you'll say so, too, you will."

The delighted mother goes on "a settin' of the table," the expectant father puts down his hat, with the air of one suddenly called upon to preside over an inquiry which will necessarily call forth all his resources, and the hopeful "Bill" having kicked the door open, is met by the emulous "Sally," book in hand.

"William, your mother says you're a good boy, and 'tend to your French. Sally, my dear, what's a kiss in French.

"A *baiser*, pa."

"A *baiser!* Let me see—'*baiser*, to kiss.' So it is. Well, then, baiser your brother, and both come here together."

"You, Bill, keep your fingers out of the pickles or I'll baiser your back for you. Kiss your sister, and go on as your pa tells you."

Bill drops the cucumber, minus one end, salutes his sister in the neighbourhood of the ear, cracks a pecan nut which he has taken from his pocket, and, with the nonchalance of a professor of languages, looks at the paternal examiner as he would say, "I guess I know more than *you* about it."

"That's right, William, always observe what your mother says to you. What is your mother in French, William?"

"She's a *mare*."

"No, brother William—a mere. M-e-r-e, mere."

"Well, I know it's m-e-r-e; but isn't the e sounded *wide*, like *a*? There's the wide accents and the sharp ones, ain't there? A great deal *you* know about it. You'd better say your father ain't a *pear!*"

"Eh?"

"Yes; I'm a *man*, you know. A man, in French?"

"Oh, yes, I know; you're a *hum*."

"No he ain't, neither; he's a *hommy*. H-o-ḿ hom, m-e me, hommy—ain't it? And a woman's a *femmy*, and a lady a *dammy*, just the same! I'm always a tellin her about the rules."

"Well, well, she's younger than you are, you know, William. What is sister in French, can you tell?"

"Yes—she's a *sewer*."

"No, Bill, I ain't. S-o-e-u-r, *sour!*"

"Well, ain't the o a *dipthorp*? and don't you drop it, say?"

"No, Bill, the e is the *dipthorp*, and that makes it *sour*."

"Massy on the children, husband, if that ain't the way they keep a disputin' from mornin' till night. There, come along, you Bill and Sally; your father can ask you all about the table things in French, you know. Come, Hubby, sit down."

"D'ye hear your mother, my dear; come to the table. Leave off your nuts, Billy; they make such a noise."

"Noise is *brute*, and nuts is *knoyx*, and table is *tabble*," screams the erudite Bill, as he draws up his chair and spoils the other end of the cucumber.

"Now, then, my dears, in the first place, *takey voo some pain*, and fill your glasses with *awe*, and your mother will help you to *hack*. *Pain* is bread, my love, and *awe* is water, amd *hack* is hash. You see, wify, I know something about it myself. Ha, Ha!"

"Well, what the world's coming to, I don't know! What with Morse's paragraph and steam chickens and learnin' one's self, I don't belong to this creation—I don't!"

"Now, William, what's that in your hand—not the pickle, the knife?"

It's a *cut-o*."

"So it is, Billy, 'cause the *dipthorp* is all sounded together at the end; and daddy was wrong about the water."—(*aside.*)

"Oh, he don't know nothin'. "—(*aside, also.*)

"The *dipthorp*, you know, Billy, is only separate when it's got a *diarhear* on top."—(*aside.*)

"Well, I know that; shut up."

"Now, husband, just let *me* ask 'em a little. Sally, what's this I'm eating now?"

"*Jaw-bane* and *choaks*, ma."

"Ba-a-ur! no it aint. She only spells—*she* can't pronounce. You're a eating *shan-bung* and *shoe!* Don't know what ham and cabbage is! Ba-a-ur!"

"Sally, my love, spelling's a great deal; but you *must* mind the pronunciation. Words don't sound at all as they look, as William shows you."

"Yes; she went and said, yesterday, that the table-cloth was a *toil* when it's *towell*, and began a crying 'cause I said a glass wasn't a *very*—Halloo! *Shovel* run away—*shovel* run away! Oh, look there, daddy—there's the *hommy* off and he's smashed his *taty* 'gainst the *pavy!* The *roo* is full of *puples*—only look—

And rushing out of the house, dragging after him the table-cloth or *towell*, as he called it, the student of French "without a master" disappeared; while his anxious parents, running to the window, beheld a horse with his head against a curb-stone, a gathering crowd, and the hopeful Billy busiest of all!

A ROLLICKING DRAGOON OFFICER.

BY "THE MAN IN THE SWAMP."

The "Spirit of the Times" has a rare correspondent in Mississippi, who signs himself the Editor's "Friend in the Swamp." He is an extraordinary genius, and has some friends who are no less "characters" in their way. Of one of them—an officer in the U. S. Dragoons—he relates the following:—

In the summer of 1834, the Dragoons went to the Pawnee Villages. In the fall, three companies under the command of Col. Kearney, came to the Des Moines Rapids, on the Mississippi, and wintered there in some log huts. There was a Captain B., a very tall man, six feet seven inches, (just three inches over me, and I think I am "some,") with very large black whiskers, a fine looking man—I wonder what has become of him? I heard that he had resigned, and settled somewhere in Iowa; he must be in Congress before this time. The captain used to boast that he could pack a gallon without its setting him back any. Sometime during the winter of '34 or '35, Col. Kearney ordered Capt. B. to repair to Rushville, Illinois, distant some sixty miles, on recruiting service. The river was closed with ice, but had the appearance of breaking up every day. There was no ferry for conveying horses at Des Moines, but there was one ten miles above, where a man by the name of Knapp kept a small store for the sale of dry goods and whisky. The captain repaired to Knapp's, and waited two or three days for the river either to freeze harder or break up; on the third morning there was no change in the river—the captain commenced early, and by nine o'clock was packing about a gallon. He ordered his horse, put his pistols in the holsters, buckled on his sword, mounted his horse, (which was a very fine one, and devilish fast for a mile,) braced himself in the stirrups, turned his horse's head for the river, and took a long look at it. Without saying a word to anybody, he gave his horse the spurs, dashed down the bank, on the ice, and crossed the river at a "quarter lick" speed. Knapp stood thunderstruck looking after him—he said he expected to see B. and the horse disappear at every jump, but they arrived safe at the other bank.

"Good Lord!" said Knapp, "I could have taken a pole and punched holes in the ice anywhere!"

"Did he look back"—I inquired—"when he reached the other side?"

"No," said Knapp, "he went up the opposite bank at the same lick, and disappeared!"

The captain arrived safe at Rushville, where he remained for several weeks, and returned without a man. He told me of some of his adventures at Rushville. He went into his favourite grocery or drinking-house, one very cold morning, and found a crowd sitting round the fire; so close were they wedged in that there was no room for another chair, if there had been one in the room. No one moved—no one offered the captain a seat. The fact is, the captain had a way of making himself unpopular with such crowds: he had an unpleasant way of using his fists when he got about a gallon on board. An old lady who lived near Des Moines, requested me to look at her husband; he was in bed, where he had been for three weeks; he was a justice of the peace, and the captain called him Chief Justice T. He said he and the captain were drinking together, and after they had become very sociable, he called him B. *without* the captain, and the next moment he was knocked into the middle of the next three weeks!

The captain had been pursuing something of the same practice at Rushville, consequently no one offered him a seat.

The captain had been a great deal about this grocery, and knew what was in every barrel, box, and keg in it. He took a good look at the crowd, and finding he was not to have a seat, he walked behind the counter, and picked up a keg marked "Dupont." He walked to the fire and threw it in, remarking—"Eternally —— my soul," [his favourite oath,] "gentlemen, if I don't think we have lived long enough!"

"Did they run?" I inquired.

"Run!" said he—"I never saw 'ground and lofty tumbling' before! They just threw themselves over backwards, and all left the house on their all-fours, some back end first, and they went in that way clear across the street!"

Hearing no explosion, they after a while ventured

back, and peeped in; there sat B., with a glass of something enjoying himself, the keg standing in one corner by him—(the keg contained madder instead of powder.) Long as the captain remained in Rushville, he had the grocery all to himself.

I wonder what has become of him? If he has not fatigued himself to death, packing a gallon at a time, he's in Congress sure.

THE GEORGIA MAJOR IN COURT.

BY A TENNESSEE EDITOR.

We are indebted to the Pulaski "Courier" for the incident subjoined in relation to that rival of "Billy Patterson," the celebrated "Georgia Major," whose exploits during the last five years have quite thrown in the shade the "deeds of high emprise" for which the far-famed "Col. Pluck" was so renowned.

His honour, the mayor, was in the discharge of his official functions on last Saturday evening—the business before him consisting of two several charges of assault and battery; to both of which our friend, the ubiquitous "Georgia major," was the respondent.

"Do you plead guilty to the charge of assaulting the Rev. Mr. Williams?" asked the mayor of the defendant.

"I do; that is to say—"

"Then I fine you ten dollars," said the mayor.

"That is to say," continued the major, "I plead guilty; but if there's any way to get off from the fine, I should like very much to do it."

"Doubtless," observed his honour.

"I will make a statement—or, as you may say, a defence—um—a-a-few remarks."

The court nodded permission.

"You see, Williams came up to me, and spoke something to me, and, said I, You d—d rascal, *pull off your hat* when you speak to me:" said the major, throwing himself into a military attitude. "That's enough—ten dollars and costs," said his honour. The major bowed gracefully.

Proceeding now to the second charge, his honour asked the defendant if he would plead guilty again. Not he! He would make a statement though, in relation, or in respect to, or regarding, the manner of the second fight.

"I was in the person's store who fought me, searching for one of the silver eyes which had dropped out of my walking cane in the previous fight, when that person ordered me out. Sir, said I, you must talk softly—*dem'd* softly when you address me, sir. Upon this, that person struck me with a skillet, sir—an *iron* skillet, sir—in the face." Here the major pointed to his face, the nasal feature of which bore some purplish streaks that beautifully varied its usual rich ruby. "And then, sir, I fell—staggered and fell, as I returned the blow with my cane. Immediately a crowd jumped upon me, and beat me 'til they were pulled off—they didn't whip me, though; *that ca-n't* be done!" Here he stopped and looked round—(by the by we thought we heard the major "holler.")

A witness being called and examined, corroborated the major's statement, except as to the crowd's having jumped upon him. No one interfered with the combatants. The witness stated, in addition, that the major had contrived to hide his head under the side of a hogshead, so as to protect it very effectually.

The major cross-examined.

"You say nobody touched me but that man?" pointing to his antagonist.

"Nobody."

"Wasn't the crowd all against me?" again asked the hero.

"The crowd thought you deserved a whipping, for striking an inoffensive man—a minister of the gospel," replied the witness very quietly.

"Didn't they all tell that man to whip me well?"

"Yes."

"And didn't he—that is—"

"Didn't he *do it*, you mean to ask? Yes he did, *nicely*."

The major now "pulled up." He had been deceived; his imagination had led him into error; completely carried him off; had transformed an individual not over the weight of a hundred and fifty pounds, into a large crowd; or at least had furnished him with Briarean facilities for a "rough and tumble scrummage."

"Well, well," said the mayor, "as I have already fined you ten dollars, and as it seems in this case you got a pretty good whipping, I reckon I must discharge you as to this."

"Whipping?" ejaculated the major, becoming positively tragic in his air; "whipping! is that a part of your sentence—that I got *whipped*? Sir, I'd rather be fined five hundred dollars than have *that* entered on the record; it *wasn't* done! I, sir, have *never* been whipped—*Angels* couldn't whip me!" And the major *loomed* majestically about the room.

"If it *ain't* been done, it *kin* be done," said somebody in the crowd—whereupon our friend collapsed into his original dimensions, in the folding of a peacock's tail; and wiping the perspiration from his brow, quietly retired.

UNCLE BILLY BROWN—"GLORIOUS!"

BY "RAMBLER," OF THE N. O. "PICAYUNE."

Whether "Rambler" is the veritable "Ex Santa Fé Prisoner" himself, or the senior of the editorial brotherhood who stand sponsors for the New Orleans "Picayune"—a sort of "child of thirty-six fathers"—we cannot undertake to decide; but the story of "Uncle Billy Brown" is "glorious," and worthy of either of them. Both Lumsden and Kendall have left their editorial sanctum for "the halls of the Montezumas," where each, we are glad to learn, has greatly distinguished himself.

"Oh, what has caused this great commotion!"

Political Song of '40.

TAKE a large stick—a fence-rail for instance—and rake it violently down a Venetian window-blind, or the side of a weather-boarded house, and you are very apt to make *some* noise, especially of a still evening.

A correspondent of ours, "Rambler," as he signs himself, says that he had just risen from the supper table of the tavern in the little village of G——, in the interior of Mississippi, one hot evening last summer, and was passing out to the front gallery to rest himself after a long day's ride, when suddenly he heard a tremendous racket as of some one raking a fence-rail down the side of a weather-boarded house, each rake followed by a shout of "glorious! glorious!" from a pair of lungs of ten trombone power. Something extra was "going on," that was certain, and tired as he was, our friend at once hobbled off towards the point whence the unwonted sounds proceeded.

He soon arrived at a door over which a light hung, and round which a score of little and big "niggers" were assembled. "What's the fun here?" was a question answered by an individual standing in the door, who said it was "a theatre." While paying for his ticket, another rake from the interior, and another "glorious!" came upon our friend's ear, accompanied this time by a loud shout as of a large political multitude assembled. He was soon inside the room, a large and long one, two-thirds of which was occupied by the audience and the remainder by the stage, leaving a small space between. It was crowded too—the benches and chairs all full—while upon the floor was seated, his arms locked around his knees and his chin nestled closely on his wrists, Uncle Billy Brown, two-thirds inebriated and the other third fast asleep.

On one side of the room, and near the row of candles which served for foot-lights, sat "the band," consisting of a large black fellow and no more, in a very high chair, a violin in his hands and a brass drum between his legs. After repeated calls for "music," he finally struck up "Hey, Jim along," playing his fiddle in the ordinary way, and with the true corn-field *abandon*, and at the same time beating a rumbling accompaniment with his knees upon the drum. This over, the bell—borrowed from the tavern after it rung the boarders in to supper—now gave signal for the curtain to rise. "Pizarro, or the Death of Rolla," got up by a Thespian corps of the town, was to be the first performance. The Peruvian appeared, and the applause was so violent that the young amateur who personated the character bowed. The applause continued, and he bowed lower. Another round, and he bowed so low that his tights gave way. A perfect earthquake of applause followed close upon the heel of this disaster, accompanied by a rake from the man with the fence-rail—it was a man with a sure-enough fence-rail—and Rolla backed out and hauled off to repair damages while the curtain was falling.

The affair so tickled the individual with the fence-rail that nothing could stop him. He raked the sides of the house, and then shouted "glorious!" and kept it up till his friends gathered round and begged him to desist. But his steam was up, and the only way he could keep from bursting was to rail and shout with all his might. A compromise was finally made with him, he agreeing if they would allow him to "make a short exhort" at the door, and "sing a hymn," he would not use his rail again unless something extra turned up.

Silence having been restored, the play was progressing towards a termination, when another interruption occurred. In one of the most affecting scenes, and while the audience sat motionless, speechless, and apparently breathless, a very large gentleman from the country rose in his seat, leaned himself forward, and fixed his gaze intently on one of the performers. Suddenly he threw out his arms, exclaiming "Good God! aint that McDonald?" Away the audience went in perfect convulsions of laughter, down came the fence-

Uncle Billy Brown "glorious" at a country theatre in Mississippi.—*Page* 113.

rail against the blinds with a rake that made all rattle again, and high above the din arose the shout of "*glorious!*" The fat man from the country heeded not the noise and commotion around him, but kept his eye fixed on the half-stupified performer. "Down in front!" came from those on the back seats, but the fat man heard not the summons. He raised his open hand over his eyes to obtain a closer sight, and bent himself still farther forward. "Why, no it aint," ejaculated he, half in doubt—"why, yes it is"—and then straightening himself, and slapping his right hand violently in his open left, he finished with "D—n me if it *isn't* McDonald sure enough." If there had been a din before, there was a perfect earthquake of noise now. The old fence-rail came down on the weather-boarding with a rake that started the nails, the shout of "*glorious!*" appeared louder from its very hoarseness, every pair of feet was stamping—every pair of hands was clapping, every throat was open and yelling, while outside the theatre the horses tied to the fences broke their bridles, and were stampeding and cavorting about amid shouts of "Stop him!" "Whoa!" "Hold my critter, there!" and similar ejaculations. Never had there been such an uproar in the little village of G——.

Order was finally restored, but only until sheer exhaustion left the audience unable to make further noisy demonstrations; and now the part enacted by the fat gentleman from the country was explained, it seemed that the Thespian's name who had attracted his attention was really McDonald. Some four months previous he had been reported dead to the fat gentleman, and as the report had never been contradicted, his bewilderment at seeing his quondam acquaintance, for he had finally made him out through all his paint, feathers, and stage trappings, led him to depart a shade from the ordinary etiquette established among theatrical audiences. He sat down, and once more the play commenced. All was hushed—a perfect quiet reigned—when suddenly it struck the fat man that he had made himself supremely ridiculous by the part he had played a few moments before. No sooner had this fancy fairly taken foothold in his mind than, in the very midst of a silence which would have become a graveyard at midnight, he laid himself back in his seat, raised both his hands above his head, and broke out with a "Ha! ha! ha!" that might have been heard a mile. Again the audience was thrown into convulsions, again the fence-rail came rattling down the sides of the house, again the shout of "*glorious!*" rose above the din, and as if this was not enough, the actors forgot Sheridan's poetry and fairly screamed in chorus—the moody and relentless Pizarro even taking a part, and laughing until the perspiration wore furrows through the red and black ferocity which rouge and burnt cork had given his countenance. It was not until exhaustion had once more got the mastery that order was restored, and the performance now went on with little interruption until "Pizarro" ended with the "Death of Rolla."

All this while, notwithstanding the din, Uncle Billy Brown had continued to snooze upon the floor; nor did the bustle attendant upon the fall of the curtain serve to raise him. The afterpiece of the "Mock Doctor" commenced, yet Uncle Billy was perfectly unconscious of what was going on around him. He was well known as the captain of a "land packet"—in plain terms, the driver of an ox-team which plied between G—— and the river towns—and but that he occasionally muttered "Gee," "Whoa," and the like, as in his dreams he imagined himself along with his team, no sounds escaped him. As the farce advanced, he gave a species of groan—a forerunner of returning consciousness—yet still he did not raise his head. The sham doctor was now proceeding to administer one of his nostrums to a patient, but the latter being backward he endeavoured to persuade him. Uncle Billy groaned again, and partially raised his head. The doctor continued his endeavours to force his drugs down his patient's throat: Uncle Billy gave still another groan, and opened his eyes. He had half-recognised the voice of the doctor, who was an old enemy of his, and entirely forgetting where he was, and imagining the Thespian endeavouring to force the vile mixture down *his* throat, he broke out with, "No—you—don't! To —— with your pills; take 'em yourself, d—n you, I don't like you, no how!"

Here was fresh and most abundant cause of uproar, and a new episode in the performance was introduced. The manager came forward and ordered that Uncle Billy be turned out—Uncle Billy drew a bowie and intimated a desire to see the chap willing to undertake the job. An assistant about the theatre grappled him, and they were soon upon the floor engaged in a regular rough-and-tumble fight. Two-thirds of the foot-lights were at once kicked over, while shouts of "Fair play," "Turn 'em out," "Give him goss," "No gouging," were heard on all sides. The ladies scrambled and scampered out, the actors mingled with the audience, the fat gentleman laughed louder than ever, Uncle Billy tusseled and swore, but high above the laughing, cursing, and swearing, arose the efforts of the rail-man. He had started off the boards on one side of the room, but having found a fresh spot he was raking away with all his might to the accompaniment of "*glorious! glorious!*"

Thus ended a theatrical performance in Mississippi. Our correspondent says that he dug his way out of the house and made the best speed he could to the tavern and to bed; but the scenes of the evening haunted him in his dreams, and several times he awoke with his hands clasped to his ears to shut out the dreadful raking of the "glorious" fellow with the fence-rail.

OLD TUTTLE'S LAST QUARTER RACE.

BY "BUCKEYE," OF OHIO.

The story annexed is the first attempt at authorship of a new Ohio correspondent of the "Spirit of the Times." He will be heard of again. We should premise that the circumstances described actually occurred in June last.

A FEW weeks since, Sol. Lauflin matched his bay four year old colt by Bacchus *vs.* Hugh's bay mare by Bacchus, also four years old, to run a quarter, in the lane near this place, for a C speck. As the colt was known to be a sharp one, and his owner "one of the b'hoys" for a quarter race, and that he also had the assistance of "Old Tuttle," (who will figure presently,) he had the call in the betting at six to four, until the day before the race, when the mare made her appearance, looking every inch a Bacchus, and fine as a star; and the owners of the old horse making a demonstration in her favour, the odds fell off, and numerous small sums were laid out at evens, up to the time of the race.

On the mounting of the riders, it appeared that the colt had the advantage in training or management, as the mare was very restive, and finally broke from her starter, and run like a scared dog, going quite through before her rider could take her up. Here the friends of the colt again rallied, and some money was laid out at five to four, p. p., but when it was known that the mare was not hurt and would start again, the odds fell off, and even was again the order of the day.

The mare was soon at her post again, and this time they got off, the mare a little in the van, which she maintains throughout, and is declared a winner by five feet! Well, there! if you ever heard a small crowd shout, you know what was done then—and if knowing ones were ever struck *speechless*, *them's they!*

Prior to the main race, or, as the play-bills have it, "previous to which," was acted the farce of "Dog eat Dog," or "The boys" *vs.* "Old Tuttle." In order to get the cream of this, you must *know* Old Tuttle—and as I am utterly unable to do him justice in a description, I'll squat, and let Hooker do it.

Look at the picture of "Simon Suggs," and you'll see Old T. physically; in the *trial* scene you find him intellectually, and in the camp-meeting scene, morally. Were it not that Old T. never "*samples*" too much when on business, and fights the "*hoss* b'hoys" instead of the "Tiger," I should say they were one and the same person. As a matter of course, a quarter race never goes off without his being *thar*—and *he* never attends without doing some *business!* So on Thursday he makes his appearance on the track, on a bay gelding, (with white hind feet,) which he calls "Indian Dick," and "allows he's as good a scrub as there'll be on the ground!" As Old T. is *known*, and Dick has been heard of, the boys are rather shy—but one of them thinks he's got a scrub that's "some pumpkins!" and would like to know, without too much cost, how far Dick can beat him; he therefore proposes to run them three hundred yards, for "sucks all round." Old T. understands the game, and says, "No, I don't want yer to treat this crowd, but I'll run with yer, just to show you *yer hoss* can't run!" This was what H. wanted, as he thought *he* could tell the speed of a horse, even though Old T. *did* ride him; so back they go to the score, and are off—with (as might be expected) H. ahead, and Old T. in the rear, whipping and spurring like mad, and letting his horse go just fast enough to put H.'s at about the top of his speed—but he can't *quite* come it—"H.'s horse is too smart, and can beat him every inch of the road." So says H., and most of the crowd are of the same opinion.

Old T. says he believes he can beat H. *Saturday*, as "Dick's shoes are loose, and heavy, and he can't run in 'em."

There was nothing more said about it till old Tut. made his appearance next morning, when the boys were all after him with "sharp sticks" and "hot bricks"—one wanted to bet him a horse on H.'s colt *vs.* his Indian Dick—another a V., another an X., and so on.

"Hold yer hosses, b'hoys! Don't all be after the old man at wunst. Wait a while and he'll commerdate yer! He's an old man, and b'lieves he knows mor'n all on yer;—but he don't want all your money at wunst. He wants to be *onabel* with yer, so he can cum agin."

This of course didn't set them back any, as they thought the old man was *scary*, and they were after him the faster. Some of the more wary cautioned them to look out, but they *didn't want no caution—they knew what they was about!* They could *beat Old Tuttle!* and they were going to "do the State some service" by skinning him. They'd make the "old cuss" poor afore they left him!

He took it all very coolly, advised some of them to

save their money for next time. He was an old man, and b'lieved he knew more'n all on 'em. *His father didn't work for nothin' sixty-five years ago!* But the boys said that was all gas, to scare them off; but 'twouldn't work! The old cuss had got to be skinned or back out.

The result was, they got up a horse and fifty dollars in money a side, to run on Saturday at two o'clock, each one to start and ride his own horse, judge tops and bottoms—the winning horse take the cakes—and no back out! Either party refusing to run forfeits the whole stakes.

Things went on smooth that day—some thinking Old T. was playing some *game* on the boys, but what the d—l it was, no one could tell. However, before night it was known there was *a secret* among the boys. They *knew* the *speed* of Dick, and *knew* they could slay him; but there mustn't any thing be said about it, as when they got the old man on the track and *right*, they were going into him the whole amount of his fixings. They'd caught the old man napping *once*. They'd got a —— sight faster horse than he thought for—and now they were going to pay off old scores.

Two o'clock came, and found Old T. on the spot, leading Dick round, and telling the boys they'd be surprised when they see Dick run his best—at the same time "doing what *business* offered"—but somehow the boys appeared a little *scary*. Old T. was "on hand" for every offer, and no mistake, and 'twas known he never bet *liberally*, unless he "had a sure thing," so that the betting soon began to lag, and the old man had the call, but no takers. Finally the old man said, "I've got a little more money, b'hoys, and I wouldn't mind giving you a chance at two to one for it." But this set them *clar back*—no one dare *bite.* There not appearing any more chance for investment, the old man stripped off his hat, coat, vest and boots, tied a red cotton bandanna around his head, (as an old man only can tie it,) then pulls off the clothes and saddle from Dick, and mounts, *bare back*, declaring himself ready.

H. mounted, and the word was given to "clear the track!" Then Old T. says, "Are yer ready?" "Yes." "Go long, then!" And over the score they go, H. a length ahead. But, oh! Jeminy! *see Dick run!* Before you could turn round twice, the ends of Old T.'s bandanna were pointing out the road for H., and at the outcome Dick was *one*, H. nowhere!

Anybody that has seen a "quarter-horse" run by a "dunghill" *knows* how this was—no one else can appreciate it. The thing was out. Old T. really knew more than all of them, sure enough—but what was the *secret*, and *how in* —— could those in the secret be so stuck? That's the idea.

The secret was, "THE BOYS" STOLE OLD TUTTLE'S HORSE on Thursday night, and run him with H.'s horse, and *beat him easy!* And the way they were stuck was this: the old man, *supposing* they would steal his horse that night, and run him, had put Dick's clothes on another horse of the same colour and marks, and about the same size, and put him in Dick's stall, starting a shoe, so that if they run him they would lose it, and he should know they had *taken the bait good.* In the morning the shoe was gone!

BILL DEAN, THE TEXAN RANGER.

BY GEO. W. KENDALL, ESQ. OF THE N. O. PICAYUNE.

In a late letter from the "seat of war" in Mexico, Kendall furnishes some capital sketches of the jokers in the army, from which we quote the following:—

Rare wags may be found among the Texas Volunteers, yet the funniest fellow of all is a happy-go-lucky chap named Bill Dean, one of Chevallier's spy company, and said to be one of the best "seven-up" players in all Texas. While at Corpus Christi, a lot of us were sitting out on the stoop of the Kinney House, early one morning, when along came Bill Dean. He did not know a single soul in the crowd, although he knew we were all bound for the Rio Grande; yet the fact that the regular formalities of an introduction had not been gone through with, did not prevent his stopping short in his walk and accosting us. His speech, or harangue, or whatever it may be termed, will lose much in the telling, yet I will endeavour to put it upon paper in as good shape as possible.

"Oh, yes," said he, with a knowing leer of the eye: "oh, yes; all going down among the robbers on the Rio Grande, are you? Fine times *you'll* have, over the left. I've been there myself, and done what a great many of you won't do—I come back: but if I did'nt see nateral h—ll,—in August at that,—I *am* a teapot. Lived eight days on one poor hawk and three blackberries—couldn't kill a prairie rat on the whole route to save us from starvation. The ninth day come, and we struck a small streak of good luck—a horse give out and broke down, plumb out in the centre of an open prairie —not a stick big enough to tickle a rattlesnake with, let alone killing him. Just had time to save the critter by shootin' him, and that was all, for in three minutes longer he'd have died a nateral death. It didn't take us long to butcher him, nor to cut off some chunks of meat and stick 'em on our ramrods; but the cookin' was another matter. I piled up a heap of prairie grass, for it was high and dry, and sot it on fire; but it flashed up like powder, and went out as quick. But—"

"But," put in one of his hearers, "but how did you cook your horse-meat after that?"

"How?"

"Yes, how?"

"Why, the fire caught the high grass close by, and the wind carried the flames streakin' across the prairie. I followed up the fire, holding my chunk of meat directly over the blaze, and the way we went it was a caution to any thing short of locomotive doin's. Once in a while a little flurry of wind would come along, and the fire would get a few yards the start; but I'd brush upon her, lap her with my chunk, and then we'd have it again, nip and chuck. You never seed such a tight race—it was beautiful."

"Very, we've no doubt," ejaculated one of the listeners, interrupting the mad wag just in season to give him a little breath: "but did you cook your meat in the end?"

"Not bad I did'nt. I chased that d——d fire a

mile and a half, the almightiest hardest race you ever heer'd tell on, and never give it up until I run her right plump into a wet marsh: there the fire and chunk of horse-meat came out even—a dead heat, especially the meat."

"But wasn't it cooked?" put in another one of the listeners.

"Cooked!—no!—just crusted over a little. You don't cook broken-down horse-flesh very easy, no how; but when it comes to chasing up a prairie fire with a chunk of it, I don't know which is the toughest, the meat or the job. You'd have laughed to split yourself to have seen me in that race—to see the fire leave me at times and then to see me brushin' up on her agin, humpin' and movin' myself as though I was runnin agin' some of those big ten mile an hour Gildersleeves in the old States. But I'm a goin over to Jack Haynes's to get a cocktail and some breakfast—I'll see you all down among the robbers on the Rio Grande."

THE STEAMBOAT CAPTAIN WHO WAS AVERSE TO RACING.

BY "THE YOUNG 'UN," OF PHILADELPHIA.

One of the most popular correspondents of the "Spirit of the Times" is "The Young 'Un"—the *nomme de plume* of a young gentleman who has lately become a resident of Philadelphia. We are not at liberty to disclose his name, but he may be seen in Chestnut street any fine day.

EARLY in the spring of the present year, a magnificent new steamer was launched upon the Ohio river, and shortly afterward made her appearance at the Levee, opposite the flourishing city of Cincinnati. Gilt-edged covers, enveloping the captain's "respects," accompanied with invitations to "see her through," upon her first trip down the river, were forwarded to the editorial corps in that vicinity; the chalked hats were "numerous" on the occasion. It was a grand affair, this *debut* of a floating palace, which has since maintained her repute untarnished as the "crack boat," *par excellence*, upon the Western waters. Your humble servant was among the "invited guests"—and a nice time he had of it!

I found myself on board this beautiful craft in "close communion" with a score of unquestionable "beauties." The company proved to be a heterogeneous conglomeration of character—made up of editors, lawyers, auctioneers, indescribables, and "fancies"—with a sprinkling of "none-such's." There was a stray parson, too, in the crowd—but as his leisure time "between meals" was spent in trading horses, we dispensed with his "grace before meals."

We left our moorings an hour before sunset, upon a clear cold afternoon, and passed rapidly down stream for a considerable distance, without experiencing any out-of-the-way occurrence. The "sons of temperance," and the parson aforesaid, amused themselves over a smoking whisky toddy—the "boys" were relieving each other of their superfluous dimes and quarters at *euchre*, when a tall gentleman, who was "some," (when he was sober,) stepped suddenly into the cabin, and imparted the information that a well-known "fast boat" had just hove in sight, at the mouth of the Kentucky river. The cards were "dropt" instanter—the punches disappeared—and the "mourners" were soon distributed in knots upon the promenade deck, to watch the progress of events.

Our "bully" boat sped away like a bird, however, and the craft behind gave us early evidence that she should offer no child's play. The "fat was in the fire" at once—a huge column of black smoke curled up in the clear atmosphere—*an extra turn or two* was visible upon our own boat, and away we went! A good deal of excitement existed among the party, as the rival steamer was clearly gaining upon us. A craft like ours, with such a company, and such a captain, musn't be *beaten*.

As the boat behind us fell in under our stern, and we could "count her passengers," a sort of impression came over us, that, by some mistake, we had got upon the wrong boat! At least, such was the expressed opinion of the parson, as he threatened to "go down *stairs*" and take another drink. Our captain was a noble fellow—he paced the deck quietly, with a constant eye to wind'ard; but he said nothing. A bevy of the mourners stepped up to him, with——

"What speed, cap'n?"

"Fair, gentlemen; I may say *very* fair."

"Smart craft, that, behind," ventured one.

"Very," responded the captain, calmly, as he placed his hand upon a small brass knob at the back of the pilot house. This movement was responded to by the faint jingling of a bell below, followed immediately by a rush of cinders from the smoke-pipes, and an improved action of the paddles.

"Now we move again."

"Some," was the response, and a momentary tremor pervaded the boat as she "slid along" right smartly.

But the craft in our rear moved like our shadow on the calm waters, and as we shot down the river, it seemed as if we had her "in tow," so calmly and uniformly did she follow in our wake. The excitement of the congregation upon deck had by this time become intense, and it was pretty plain that the boats must shortly part company, or "split something!" The rascal behind us took advantage of a turn in the channel, and "helm a-starboard!" was clearly heard from the look-out of our rival, as she "hove off," and suddenly fell alongside us! The parson went below at once, to put his threat into execution, as we came up into the current again, "neck and neck;" and when he returned we were running a twenty-five-knot lick, the steam smack on to 49°!

"She's going—goin' go——," muttered an auctioneer to himself.

"A perfect nonsuit," remarked a lawyer.

"Beaten, but not vanquished," added a politician; and away we scudded side by side for half a mile.

"Wouldn't she bear a *leetle* more?" meekly asked the parson.

"She's doing very well," replied the captain. "Don't get excited, gentlemen; my boat is a new one—her reputation and mine is at stake. We musn't rush her—*racing always injures a boat*, and I am averse to it;" saying which he applied his thumb and finger to the brass knob again—the bell tinkled in the distance—and our rival pilot shortly had an opportunity to examine the architecture of our rudder-post!

I was acquainted with the engineer. I stepped below, (believing we should be beaten at our present speed,) and entering the engine-room—

"Tim," said I, "we'll be licked—give her another turn, eh?"

"I raythar think she moves *some* as it is," said Tim.

"Yes: but the C—— is hard on us—give her a little, my boy—just for——"

"Step in here a moment," remarked Tim; "it's all 'mum,' you know—nothin to be said, eh? Quiet—there!—don't she tremble some?"

I noticed, for the first time, that our boat did labour prodigiously!

"But come round *here*," continued Tim: "*look there!—mum's* the word you know."

I stepped out of that engine-room (Tim said afterwards, that I "sprang out at one bound;" but he lied!) in a hurry. *The solder upon the connection-pipe had melted and run down over the seams in a dozen places*, from the excessive heat—a crow-bar was braced athwart the safety-valve, with a "fifty-six" upon one end—and we were shooting down the Ohio, under a head of steam "chock up" to 54 40!!

My "sleeping apartment" was well aft. I entered the state-room—got over upon the *back* side of my berth—and, stuffing the corners of the pillow into my ears, endeavoured to compose myself in sleep. It was out of the question. In attempting to "right myself," I discovered that *my hair stuck out so straight, it was impossible for me to get my head within six inches of the pillow!*

I tossed about till daylight, in momentary expectation of being landed in Kentucky, (or somewhere else!) but we got on finely. We led our rival half an hour into Louisville; and I immediately swore upon my nightcap that I would never accept another invitation, for a pleasure trip, from *a steamboat captain who was averse to racing!*

BOB HERRING, THE ARKANSAS BEAR HUNTER.

BY T. B. THORPE, ESQ., OF NEW ORLEANS.

As the author of "The Mysteries of the Backwoods," and a series of sporting sketches in the "Spirit of the Times," of which "The Big Bear of Arkansas," and "Tom Owen, the Bee Hunter," are perhaps best known, Mr. Thorpe has acquired the most enviable reputation on both sides of the Atlantic. It is not so generally known that he is, by profession, a painter; and his abilities as an artist are cheerfully acknowledged by his contemporaries. Since the breaking out of the war with Mexico, Thorpe has visited its theatre, and the result has been a very interesting volume, containing many illustrations from drawings by himself, made on the spot. It is called "Our Army of Occupation;" the publishers were Carey & Hart, of Philadelphia; and the work may be obtained at any book-store for half-a-dollar, though worth five times that amount.

It is not expected that a faithful description of the Devil's Summer Retreat, in Arkansas, will turn the current of fashion of two worlds, from Brighton and Bath, or from Ballston or Saratoga, although the residents in the neighbourhood of that delightful place profess to have ocular demonstration, as well as popular opinion, that his Satanic Majesty, in warm weather, regularly retires to the "retreat," and "there reclines in the cool." The solemn grandeur that surrounds this distinguished resort is worthy of the hero, as represented by Milton; its characteristics are darkness, gloom, and mystery; it is composed of the unrivalled vegetation and forest of the Mississippi Valley. View it when you will, whether decked out in all the luxuriance of a southern summer, or stripped of its foliage by the winter's blasts; it matters not, its grandeur is always sombre. The huge trees seem immortal, their roots look as if they struck to the centre of the earth, while the gnarled limbs reached out to the clouds. Here and there may be seen one of these lordly specimens of vegetation furrowed by the lightning; from its top to the base you can trace the subtle fluid in its descent, and see where it shattered off the limb, larger than your body, or turned aside from some slight inequality in the bark. These stricken trees, no longer able to repel the numerous parasites that surround them, soon become festooned with wreaths and flowers, while the damp airs engender on living tree and dead, like funeral drapery, the pendant moss, that waves in every breeze, and seems to cover the whole scene with the gloom of the grave. Rising out of this forest for ten square miles, is the dense cane-brake that bears the name of the "Devil's Summer Retreat;" it is formed by a space of ground, on which, seemingly from its superiority of soil, more delicate vegetation than surrounds it has usurped its empire. Here the reed, that the disciple of Izaak Walton plays over the northern streams like a wand, grows into a delicate mast, springing from the rich alluvium that gives it sustenance with the prodigality of grass, and tapering from its roots to the height of twenty or thirty feet, there mingling, in com pact and luxuriant confusion, its long leaves. A portion of this brake is interwoven with vines of all descriptions, which makes it so thick that it seems to be impenetrable as a mountain. Here, in this solitude, where the noon-day sun never penetrates, ten thousand birds, with the instinct of safety, roost at night, and at the dawn of day, for a while, darken the air as they seek their haunts, their manure deadening, for acres round, the vegetation, like a fire, so long have they possessed the solitude. Around this mass of cane and vine, the black bears retire for winter quarters, where they pass the season, if not disturbed, in the insensibility of sleep, and yet come out in the spring as fat as when they commenced their long nap. The forest, the waste, and the dangers of the cane brake, add to the excitement of the Arkansas hunter; he conquers them all, and makes them subservient to his pursuits. Associated with these scenes, they to him possess no sentiment; he builds his log cabin in a clearing made by his own hands, amid the surrounding grandeur, and it looks like a gipsy hut among the ruins of a Gothic cathedral. The noblest trees are only valuable for fence-rails, and the cane-brake is "an infernal dark hole," where you can "see sights," "catch bears," and "get a fish-pole, ranging in size from a penny whistle to that of a young stove-pipe."

The undoubted hero of the Devil's Summer Retreat, is old Bob Herring; he has a character that would puzzle three hundred metaphysicians consecutively. He is as bold as a lion, and as superstitious as an Indian. The exact place of his birth he cannot tell, as he says his parents "travelled" as long as he can remember them. He "squatted" on the Mississippi, at its nearest point to the Retreat, and there erecting a rude cabin commenced hunting for a living, having no prospect ahead but selling out his "pre-emption right" and improvements, and again squatting somewhere else. Unfortunately the extent of Arkansas, and the swamp that surrounded Bob's location, kept it out of market, until, to use his own language, he "became the ancientest inhabitant in the hull of Arkansaw." And having, in spite of himself, gradually formed acquaintances with the few residents in this vicinity, and grown into importance from his knowledge of the country and his hunting exploits, he has established himself for life, at what he calls the "Wasp's diggins," made a potato patch, which he has never had time to fence in, talked largely of a corn-field, and hung his cabin round with rifle pouches, gourds, red-peppers, and flaming advertisements with rampant horses and pedigrees; these latter ornaments he looks upon as rather sentimental, but he excuses himself on the ground that they look "hoss," and he considers such an expression as considerably resembling himself. We have stated that Bob's mind would puzzle three hundred metaphysicians consecutively, and we as boldly assert that an equal number of physiologists would be brought to a stand by his personal appearance. The left side of his face is good looking, but the right side seems to be under the influence of an invisible air-pump; it looks sucked out of shape; his perpendicular height is six feet one inch, but that gives the same idea of his length, that the diameter gives of the circumference; how long Bob Herring would be if he was drawn out, is impossible to tell. Bob himself says, that he was made on too tall a scale for this world, and that he was shoved in, like the joints of a telescope. Poor in flesh, his enormous bones and joints rattle when he moves, and they would no doubt have long since fallen apart, but for the enormous tendons that bind them together as visibly as a good-sized hawser would. Such is Bob Herring, who on a bear hunt will do more hard work, crack more jokes, and be more active than any man living, sustaining the whole with unflinching good humour, never getting angry except when he breaks his whisky bottle, or has a favourite dog open on the wrong trail.

My first visit to the Devil's Summer Retreat was propitious, my companions were all choice spirits, the weather was fine, and Bob Herring inimitable. The bustling scene that prefaced the "striking the camp" for night lodgings, was picturesque and animated; a long ride brought us to our halting place, and there was great relief in again stepping on the ground. Having hobbled our horses, we next proceeded to build a fire, which was facilitated by taking advantage of a dead tree for a back-log; our saddles, guns, and other necessaries were brought within the circle of its light, and lolling upon the ground we partook of a frugal supper, the better to be prepared for our morrow's exertions, and our anticipated breakfast. Beds were next made up, and few can be better than a good supply of cane tops, covered with a blanket, with a saddle for a pillow; upon such a rude couch, the hunter sleeps more soundly than the effeminate citizen on his down. The crescent moon, with her attendant stars, studded the canopy under which we slept, and the blazing fire completely destroyed the chilliness of a southern December night.

The old adage of "early to bed and early to rise," was intended to be acted upon, that we might salute the tardy sun with the heat of our sport, and probably we would have carried out our intentions had not Bob Herring very coolly asked if any of us snored "unkimmonly loud," for he said his old shooting iron would go off at a good imitation of a bear's breathing! This sally from Bob brought us all upright, and then there commenced a series of jibes, jokes, and stories, that no one can hear, or witness, except on an Arkansas hunt with "old coons." Bob, like the immortal Jack, was witty himself, and the cause of wit in others, but he sustained himself against all competition, and gave in his notions and experience with an unrivalled humour and simplicity. He found in me an attentive listener, and went into details, until he talked every one but myself asleep. From general remarks, he changed to addressing me personally, and as I had every thing to learn, he went from the elementary to the most complex experience. "You are green in bar hunting," said he to me, in a commiserating tone, and with a toss of the head that would have done honour to Mr. Brummel in his glory; "green as a jinson weed—but don't get short-winded 'bout it, case it's a thing like readin', to be larnt;—a man don't come it parfectly at once, like a dog does; and as for that, they larn a heap in time;—thar is a greater difference 'tween a pup and an old dog on a bar hunt than thar is 'tween a malitia man and a riglar. I remember when I couldn't bar hunt, though the thing seems onpossible now; it only requires time, a true eye, and steady hand, though I did know a fellow that called himself a doctor, that said that couldn't do it if you was narvious. I asked him if he meant by that agee and fever? He said it was the agee without the fever. Thar may be such a thing as narvious, stranger, but nothin' but a yarthquake, or the agee, can shake me; and still bar hunting ain't as easy as scearing a wild turkey, by a long shot. The varmint aint a hog, to run with a w—h—e—w; just corner one—cotch its cub, or cripple it, and if you don't have to fight, or get out of the way, then thar ain't no cat-fish in the Mississip. I larnt that, nigh twenty year ago, and perhaps you would like to know about it." Signifying my assent, Bob Herring got up in his bed, for as it was the bare ground he could not well get off of it, and approaching the fire, he threw about a cord of wood on it, in the form of a few huge logs; as they struck the blazing heap the sparks flew upwards in the clear cold air, like a jet of stars; then fixing himself comfortably, he detailed what follows:—

"I had a knowing old sow at that time that would have made a better hunter than any dog ever heerd on; she had such a nose,—talk 'bout a dog following a cold trail, she'd track a bar through running water. Well, you see, afor' I know'd her vartu', she came rushing into my cabin, bristles up, and fell on the floor, from what I now believe to have been regular sceare. I thought she'd seen a bar, for nothing else could make her run; and taking down my rifle, I went out a sort a carelessly, with only two dogs at my heels. Hadn't gone far afore I saw a bar, sure enough, very quietly standing beside a small branch—it was an old *he*, and no mistake. I crawled up to him on my hands and knees, and raised my rifle, but if I had fired I must have hit him so far in front, that the ball would have ranged back, and not cut his mortals. I waited, and he turned tail towards me, and started across the branch; afeerd I'd lose him, I blazed away, and sort a cut him slantindicularly through his hams, and brought him down; thar he sat, looking like a sick nigger with the dropsy, or a black bale of cotton turned up on eend. 'Twas not a judgmatical shot, and Smith thar" (pointing at one of the sleeping hunters) "would say so." Hereupon Bob Herring, without ceremony, seized a long stick, and thrust it into Smith's short ribs, who, thus suddenly awakened from a sound sleep, seized his knife, and looking about him, asked, rather confusedly, what was the matter? "Would you," inquired Bob, very leisurely, "would you, under any circumstances, shoot an old *he* in the hams?" Smith very peremptorily told his questioner to go where the occupier of the Retreat in Summer is supposed to reside through the winter months, and went instantly to sleep again. Bob continued,—"Stranger, the bar, as I have said, was on his hams, and thar he sot, waiting to whip somebody and not knowing whar to begin, when the two dogs that followed me came up, and pitched into him like a caving bank. I knowed the result afor the fight began; Brusher had his whole scalp, ears and all, hanging over his nose in a minute, and Tig was laying some distance from the bar, on his back, breathing like a horse with the thumps; he wiped them both out with one stroke of his left paw, and thar he sot, knowing as well as I did, that he was not obliged to the dogs for the hole in his carcass, and thar I stood, like a fool, rifle in hand, watching him, instead of giving him another ball. All of a sudden he caught a glimpse of my hunting shirt, and the way he walked at me with his two fore legs was a caution to slow dogs. I instantly fired, and stepped round behind the trunk of a large tree; my second shot confused the bar, and he was hunting about for me, when, just as I was patching my ball, he again saw me, and, with his ears nailed back to his head, he gave the d——t w—h—e—w I ever heerd, and made straight at me; I leaped up a bank near by, and as I gained the top my foot touched the eend of his nose. If I ever had the 'narvious' that was the time, for the skin on my face seemed an inch thick, and my eyes had more rings in them than a mad wild-cat's. At this moment several of my dogs, that war out on an expedition of their own, came up, and immediately made battle with the bar, who shook off the dogs in a flash, and made at me agin; the thing was done so quick, that, as I raised my rifle, I stepped back and fell over, and thinking my time was come, wished I had been born to be hung, and not chaw'd up; but the bar didn't cotch me: his hind quarters, as he came at me, fell into a hole about a root, and caught. I was on my feet, and out of his reach in a wink, but as quick as I did this he had cut through a green root the size of my leg: he did it in about two snaps, but weakened by the exertion, the dogs got hold of him, and held on while I blowed his heart out. Ever since that time I have been wide awake with a wounded bar—*sartinly, or stand off* being my motto. I shall dream of that bar to-night,' concluded Bob, fixing his blanket over him; and a few moments only elapsed before he was in danger of his life, if his rifle would go off at a good imitation of a bear's breathing.

Fortunately for me, the sun on the following morn was fairly above the horizon before our little party was ready for the start. While breakfast was being prepared, the rifles were minutely examined; some were taken apart, and every precaution used to ensure a quick and certain fire. A rude breakfast having been despatched, lots were drawn, who should go into the *drive* with the dogs, as this task in the Devil's Summer Retreat is any thing but a pleasant one, being obliged at one time to walk on the bending cane—it is so thick for hundreds of yards that you cannot touch or see the ground—then crawling on your hands and knees, between its roots, sometimes brought to a complete halt, and obliged to cut your way through with your knife. While this is going on, the hunters are at *the stands*, places their judgments dictate as most likely to be passed by the bear, when roused by the dogs. Two miles might on this occasion have been passed over by those in the drive, in the course of three hours, and yet, although "signs were plenty as leaves," not a bear was started. Hard swearing was heard, and as the vines encircled the feet, or caught one under the nose, it was increased. In the midst of this ill humour, a solitary bark was heard; some one exclaimed, that was Bose! another shrill yelp that sounded like Music's; breathing was almost suspended in the excitement of the moment;

presently another, and another bark, was heard in quick succession, in a minute more, *the whole pack of thirty-five staunch dogs opened!* The change from silence to so much noise made it almost deafening. No idea but personal demonstration can be had of the effect upon the mind, of such a pack baying a bear in a cane-break. Before me were old hunters; they had been moving along, as if destitute of energy or feeling, but now their eyes flashed, their lips were compressed, and their cheeks flushed; they seemed incapable of fatigue. As for myself, my feelings almost overcame me, I felt a cold sweat stealing down my back, my breath was thick and hot, and as I suspended it, to hear more distinctly the fight, for by this time the dogs had evidently come up with the bear, I could hear the pulsation of my heart. One minute more to listen, to learn which direction the war was raging, and then our party unanimously sent forth a yell that would have frightened a nation of Indians. The bear was in his bed when the dogs first came up with him, and he did not leave it until the pack surrounded him; then finding things rather too warm, he broke off with a "whew" that was awful to hear. His course was towards us on the left, and as he went by, the cane cracked and smashed as if rode over by an insane locomotive. Bob Herring gave the dogs a salute as they passed, close at the bear's heels, and the noise increased, until he said "it sounded as if all h——l was pounding bark." The bear was commented on as he rushed by; one said he was "a buster." "A regular built eight years old," said another. "Fat as a candle," shouted a third. "He's the beauty of the Devil's Summer Retreat, with a band of angels after him," sang out

Bob Herring. On the bear plunged, so swiftly that our greatest exertions scarcely enabled us to keep within hearing distance; his course carried him towards those at the stands, but getting wind of them, he turned and exactly retraced his course, but not with the same speed; want of breath had already brought him several times to a stand, and a fight with the dogs. He passed us the second time within two hundred yards, and coming against a fallen tree, backed up against it, and showed a determination, if necessary, there to die. We made our way towards the spot, as fast as the obstacles in our way would let us, the hunters anxious to despatch him, that as few dogs as possible might be sacrificed. The few minutes to accomplish this seemed months, the fight all the time sounding terrible, for every now and then the bear evidently made a rush at the dogs, as they narrowed their circle, or came individually too near his person. Crawling through and over the cane-brake was a new thing to me, and in the prevailing excitement, my feet seemed tied together, and there *was always a vine directly under my chin*, to cripple my exertions. While thus struggling, I heard a suspicious cracking in my rear, and looking round, I saw Bob Herring, a foot taller than common, stalking over the cane, like a colossus; he very much facilitated my progress, by a shove in the rear. "Come along, stranger," he shouted, his voice as clear as a bell, "Come along, the bar and the dogs are going it, like a high pressure nigger camp-meeting, and I must be thar to put a word in sartin." Fortunately for my wind, I was nearer the contest than I imagined, for Bob Herring stopped just ahead of me, examined his rifle with two or three other hunters, just arrived from the stands, and by peeping through the under-growth, we discovered, within thirty yards of us, the fierce raging fight. Nothing distinctly, however, was seen; a confused mass of legs, heads, and backs of dogs, flying about as if attached to a ball, was all we could make out. A still nearer approach, and the confusion would clear off for a moment, and the head of the bear could be seen, with his tongue covered with dust, and hanging a foot from his mouth; his jaws were covered with foam and blood, his eyes almost protruding from their sockets, while his ears were so closely pressed to the back of his head, that he seemed destitute of those appendages; the whole indicative of unbounded rage and terror.

These glimpses of the bear were only momentary; his persecutors rested but for a breath, and then closed in, regardless of their own lives, for you could discover, mingled with the sharp bark of defiance, the yell that told of death. It was only while the bear was crushing some luckless dog, that they could cover his back, and lacerate it with their teeth. One of the hunters, in spite of the danger, headed by Bob Herring, crept upon his knees, so near that it seemed as if another foot advanced would bring them within the circle of the fight. Bob Herring was first within safe shooting distance to save the dogs, and waving his hand to those behind him, he raised his rifle and sighted, but his favourite dog, impatient for the report, anticipated it by jumping on the bear, who throwing up his head at the same instant, the bear received the ball in his nose. At the crack of the rifle, the well-trained dogs, thinking less caution than otherwise necessary, jumped pell-mell on the bear's back, and the hardest fight ever witnessed in the Devil's Summer Retreat ensued; the hunter, with Bob, placed his gun almost against the bear's side, and the cap snapped; no one else was near enough to fire without hitting the dogs.—" Give him the knife!" cried those at a distance. Bob Herring's long blade was already flashing in his hand, but sticking a living bear is not child's play; he was standing undecided, when he saw the hind legs of Bose upwards; thrusting aside one or two of the dogs with his hand, he made a pass at the bear's throat, but the animal was so quick, that he struck the knife with his fore paw, and sent it whirling into the distant cane; another was instantly handed him, which he thrust at the bear, but the point was so blunt that it would not penetrate the skin. Foiled a third time, with a tremendous oath on himself and the owner of the knife "that wouldn't stick a cabbage," he threw it indignantly from him, and seizing, unceremoniously, a rifle, just then brought up by one of the party, heretofore in the rear, he, regardless of his own legs, thrust it against the side of the bear with considerable force, and blowed him through; the bear struggled but for a moment, and fell dead, "I saw snakes last night in my dreams," said Bob, handing back the rifle to its owner, "and I never had any good luck the next day, arter sich a sarcumstance; I call this hull hunt about as mean an affair as damp powder; that bar thar," pointing to the carcass, "that thar, ought to have been killed, afor he maimed a dog." Then, speaking energetically, he said, "Boys, never shoot at a bar's head, even if your iron is in his ear, it's unsartin; look how I missed the brain, and only tore the smellers; with fewer dogs, and sich a shot, a fellow would be ripped open in a powder flash; and I say, cuss caps, and head shooting; they would have cost two lives to-day, but for them ar dogs, God bless 'em."

With such remarks, Bob Herring beguiled away the time, while he, with others, skinned the bear. His huge carcass, when dressed, though not over fat, looking like a young steer's. The dogs, as they recovered breath, partook of the refuse with relish; the nearest possible rout out of the Devil's Retreat was selected, and two horse loads took the meat into the open woods, where it was divided out in such a manner that it could be taken home. Bob Herring, while the dressing of the bear was going on, took the skin, and on its inside surface, which glistened like satin, he carefully deposited the caul fat, that looked like drifted snow, and beside it the liver; the choice parts of the bear, according to the gourmand notions of the frontier, were in Bob's possession; and many years' experience had made him so expert in cooking it, that he was locally famed for this matter above all competitors. It would be as impossible to give the recipe for this dish, so that it might be followed by the gastronomes of cities, as it would to have the articles composing it exposed for sale in the markets. Bob Herring managed as follows: he took a long wooden skewer, and having thrust its point through a small piece of bear fat, he then followed it by a small piece of the liver, then the fat, then the liver, and so on, until his most important material was consumed; when this was done, he opened the "bear's handkerchief," or caul, and wrapped it round the whole, and thus roasted it before the fire. Like all the secrets in cookery, this dish depends for its flavour and richness upon exactly giving the proper quantities, as a superabundance of one or the other would completely spoil the dish. "I was always unlucky, boys," said Bob, throwing the bear skin and its contents over his shoulder, "but I've had my fill often of caul fat and liver; many a man, who thinks he's *lucky*, lives and dies ignorant of its virtue, as a 'possum is of corn cake. If I ever look dead don't bury me until you see I don't open my eyes when its ready for eating; if I don't move when you show me it, then I am a done goner, sure." Night closed in before we reached our homes, the excitement of the morning wore upon our spirits and energy, but the evening's meal of caul fat and liver, and other similar "fixins," or Bob Herring's philosophical remarks, restored me to perfect health, and I shall recollect that supper, and its master of ceremonies, as harmonious with, and as extraordinary as is, the Devil's Summer Retreat.

M[c]ALPIN'S TRIP TO CHARLESTON.

BY THE AUTHOR OF "COUSIN SALLY DILLIARD."

The writer of the following "good 'un" is an eminent member of the North Carolina bar. He has lately furnished the "Spirit of the Times" with a number of original stories, from which the one annexed is selected as a specimen of his style:—

In the county of Robison, in the state of North Carolina, there lived in times past a man by the name of Brooks, who kept a grocery for a number of years, and so had acquired most of the land round him. This was mostly pine barrens, of small value, but nevertheless Brooks was looked up to as a great landholder and big man in the neighbourhood. There was one tract, however, belonging to one Colonel Lamar, who lived in Charleston, that "*jammed in upon him so strong*," and being withal better in quality than the average of his own domain, that Brooks had long wished to add it to his other broad acres. Accordingly he looked around him and employed, as he expressed it, "the smartest man in the neighbourhood," to wit, one Angus McAlpin, to go to Charleston and negotiate with Colonel Lamar for the purchase of this also. Being provided pretty well with bread, meat, and a bottle of *pale-face*, which were stowed away in a pair of leather saddle-bags, and, like all other great *Plenipotentiaries*, being provided with suitable instructions, Mac mounted a piney-wood-tacky (named Rosum) and hied him off to Charleston. The road was rather longer than Brooks had supposed, or his agent was less expeditious, or some bad luck had happened to him, or something was the matter that Angus did not get back until long after the day had transpired which was fixed on for his return. Brooks in the mean time had got himself into a very fury of impatience. He kept his eyes fixed on the Charleston road—he was crusty towards his customers—harsh towards his wife and children, and scarcely eat or slept for several days and nights, for he had set his whole soul upon buying the Lamar land. One day, however, Angus was descried slowly and sadly wending his way up the long stretch of sandy road that made up to the grocery. Brooks went out to meet him, and, without further ceremony, he accosted him.

"Well, Mac, have you got the land?"

The agent, in whose face was any thing but sunshine, replied somewhat gruffly that "he might let a body get down from his horse before he put at him with questions of business."

But Brooks was in a fever of anxiety and repeated the question—

"Did you get it?"

"Shaw, now, Brooks, don't press upon a body in this uncivil way. It is a long story and I must have time."

Brooks still urged, and Mac still parried the question till they got into the house.

"Now, surely," thought Brooks, "he will tell me." But Mac was not quite ready.

"Brooks," says he, "have you any thing to drink?"

"To be sure I have," said the other, and immediately

had some of his best forth-coming. Having moistened his clay, Mac took a seat and his employer another. Mac gave a preliminary hem! He then turned suddenly around to Brooks, looked him straight in the eyes, and slapped him on the thigh—

"Brooks," says he, "was you ever in Charleston?"

"Why, you know I never was," replied the other.

"Well, then, Brooks," says the agent, "you ought to go there. The greatest place upon the face of the earth! They've got houses there on both sides of the road for five miles at a stretch, and d——n the horse-track the whole way through! Brooks, I think I met five thousand people in a minute, and not a chap would look at me. They have got houses there on wheels. Brooks! I saw one with six horses hitched to it, and a big driver with a long whip going it like a whirlwind. I followed it down the road for a mile and a half, and when it stopt I looked, and what do you think there was? nothing in it but one little woman sitting up in one corner. Well, Brooks, I turned back up the road, and as I was riding along I sees a fancy looking chap with long curly hair hanging down his back, and his boots as shiney as the face of an up-country nigger! I called him into the middle of the road and asked him a civil question; and a civil question, you know, Brooks, calls for a civil answer all over the world. I says, says I, 'Stranger, can you tell me where Colonel Lamar lives?' and what do you think was his answer—'*Go to h——l, you fool!*'

"Well, Brooks, I knocks along up and down and about, until at last I finds out where Colonel Lamar lived. I gets down and bangs away at the door.

Presently the door was opened by as pretty, fine-spoken, well-dressed a woman as ever you seed in your born days, Brooks. *Silk!* Silks *thar* every day, Brooks! Says I, 'Mrs. Lamar, I presume, madam,' says I. 'I am Mrs. Lamar, sir.' 'Well, madam,' says I, 'I have come all the way from North Carolina to see Colonel Lamar—to see about buying a tract of land from him that's up in our parts?' 'Then,' she says, 'Colonel Lamar has rode out in the country, but will be back shortly. Come in, sir, and wait a while. I've no doubt the colonel will soon return,' and she had a smile upon that pretty face of her's that reminded a body of a Spring morning. Well, Brooks, I hitched my horse to a brass thing on the door, and walked in. Well, when I got in I sees the floor all covered over with the nicest looking thing! nicer than any patched-worked bed-quilt you ever seed in your life, Brooks. I was trying to edge along round it, but presently I sees a big nigger come stepping right over it. Thinks I, if that nigger can go it, I can go it, too! So right over it I goes and takes my seat right before a picture, which at first I thought was a little man looking in at the window. Well, Brooks, there I sot waiting and waiting for Colonel Lamar, and *at* last—he didn't come, but they began to bring in dinner. Thinks I to myself, here's a scrape. But I made up my mind to tell her, if she axed me to eat—to tell her with a genteel bow that I *had no occasion to eat.* But, Brooks, she didn't ax me to eat—she axed me if I'd be so good as to carve that turkey for her, and she did it with one of them lovely smiles that makes the cold streaks run down the small of a feller's back. 'Certainly, madam,' says I, and I walks up to the table—there was on one side of the turkey a great big knife as big as a bowie knife, and a fork with a trigger to it on the other side. Well, I falls to work, and in the first *e*-fort I slashed the gravy about two yards over the whitest table-cloth you ever seed in your life, Brooks! Well! I felt the hot steam begin to gather about my cheeks and eyes. But I'm not a man to back out for trifles, so I makes another *e*-fort, and the darned thing took a flight and lit right in Mrs. Lamar's lap! Well, you see, Brooks, then I was taken with a blindness, and the next thing I remember I was upon the *hath* a-kicking. Well, by this time I began to think of navigating. So I goes out and mounts Rosum, and cuts for North Carolina! Now, Brooks, you don't blame me! Do you?"

INDIA RUBBER PILLS.

BY "CHEVAL," OF PHILADELPHIA.

The following anecdote of a "Down-East" quack doctor was furnished by a young gentleman who has just made his *debut* as a correspondent of the "Spirit of the Times." He promises to be "one of 'em."

In the manufacturing city of L——, there lives a certain Dr. D——. Not that he has a legitimate title to write M. D. behind his name; but all who know him are conscious that he deserves something more than plain Mister, and as he is a chemist and druggist by profession, common consent has established the "Doctor."

Were I to attempt to describe the doctor as he merits, you would be compelled to issue an extra, but I cannot resist the opportunity of giving him a "passing notice." In the first place, he is a "universal genius." He does every thing he undertakes better than any one else can. Nothing comes amiss to him, from a pill to a porcelain tooth—from a lotion to a landscape—from a draught to a drawing. A—— W——, Esq., has among his collection of pictures a couple of landscapes painted by the doctor, which would do credit to the cabinet of any gentleman in the country. In short, were he a Yankee, he knows enough to revolutionize half the world.

Some years ago, about the time we began to discover that India rubber could be put to other uses besides making over-shoes and erasing pencil-marks, our doctor prepared a compound of the article, which could be applied to either leather or cloth, making it "as impervious to water as a drunkard's throat." Accommodating himself to the universal taste for *humbug*, he hung, on the outside of his shop, large placards headed—

"BEWARE OF COLDS, COUGHS, AND CONSUMPTION."

Underneath was a long description of the evils and ills consequent upon getting *wet feet;* all of which were to be avoided by using Dr. D——'s "celebrated compound."

The mixture was put up in small boxes, neatly labelled, and much resembling many "patent medicines."

One "sloppy day" in March, a tall, lanky, factory girl, just fresh from "Varmount," came splashing along through the snow and water, coughing at every step as though she were on her way to make a bargain with the sexton. The placards caught her eye, and she read one through with open-mouthed attention. When finished, she stepped into the shop, and bought a box of the mixture, being served by the doctor in person.

A few days after, the doctor was standing behind his counter, outside of which were two or three of his friends. In came the same girl, coughing, if possible, more than before, and the following dialogue ensued. I must here remark that our friend the doctor is rather "gruff" in look, and oftentimes rough in manner and speech, although a better-hearted being never breathed.

"See here," said the girl, as well as she could for coughing, "I warnt you to take back this stuff of yourn, 'taint good for nothin'."

"'Taint good for nothin'," replied the doctor, imitating her, for he was touched on a tender point. "What does the girl mean? Let me see the box."

The box was produced and opened, when there appeared to have been a small portion scooped out, something as it might have been done by one's thumb nail.

"Why," said the doctor, "how can you tell that '*the stuff aint good for nothin'*,' when you have not used one quarter the proper quantity?"

"I took as much as I darst tu," answered the girl, "and as much as the rest of the gals said would be enuff."

"*Took!*" almost shouted the doctor—"Took! What do you mean by *taking?* How did you *take* it?"

"Why, sir," said the girl, "I didn't know what to do with it myself, so I asked the other gals, and they said I must make it into pills. I took four when I went tu bed, and the next mornin' I coughed worser than ever."

"Humph!" growled the doctor, at the same time handing the girl back her money. "*Took it*, did ye, in the shape of pills? Well, if you aren't *water-tight* for the balance of your life, I'm blowed!"

The poor girl sloped just in time to prevent the doctor's friends from expiring.

A MURDER CASE IN MISSISSIPPI.

BY AN ASSOCIATE EDITOR OF THE N. O. "DELTA."

One of the best diurnals published south of "Mason & Dixon's Line," is the New Orleans "Daily Delta," of Messrs. Davis, Corcoran, & Hayes. To which of them we are indebted for the following "good thing," deponent saith not; we confess judgment, however, that we "owe him one."

While sojourning for a few days, about the period of the solstice last summer, in one of the marine villages of the state of Mississippi, that skirt the Mexican Gulf, an event transpired which, for a time—a brief time only—started the hamlet from its propriety. We shall proceed to give a hurried sketch of the occurrence, with the view of giving it typical notoriety.

The sun, on the morning of the day to which we are about to refer, rose from the Gulf with a rosy glow, and ere long flung forth its rays, polishing its surface, as though it were a "monster" mirror. Bilious-looking, liver-affected gentlemen, in broad-brimmed Panama and Leghorn hats, and morning gowns; young ladies in sun bonnets and "Nora creena" dresses; and older ladies in no particular style of dress, might be seen wending their way up to the hotel, having taken their matin ablution. The birds in the neighbouring pine-trees had given their first concert for the morning; the sun was fast beginning to absorb the little, crystallized, globular dew drops, which, a short time before, surmounted the grass blades, making the lawn in front of the hotel look like an enamelled carpet, ornamented with spangles. Dissipated-looking gentlemen might also be observed, hurriedly preparing their toilet for breakfast, and little else was to be heard than a call for "boots" from No. 5—a call for soap from No. 9, or a call for a napkin from No. 13, except the hissing of the fish, as, half covered in butter, they fried in the kitchen.

While things were in a state such as we have represented them, a tall, thin man, with the nether ends of his trousers thrust into the legs of his horse-skin boots, without any coat, unshaven, and wearing an old cone-crowned, gray, woollen hat, walked hurriedly and agitatedly up to where a group of boarders was standing at the hotel door, and inquired for the attorney of the district, who happened to be standing at the hotel at the time. The latter functionary having heard his name mentioned, walked out from his room and asked "Jones"—the man in the horse-skin boots—"What the d——l are you after so early?—Court don't sit till ten."

Now Jones, knowing that to answer this very familiar, though not very polite interrogatory, he would have to open his mouth, and knowing that in opening his mouth he could not retain the quantity of tobacco juice with which it was filled, took the preliminary precaution to expectorate it, before replying to the learned district attorney; which done, he told him in a half-mysterious, half-astonished tone, that "it was done at last."

"Jones," says the district attorney, "you're a living note of admiration!"—and Jones, by the way, did not look unlike a standing one. "You're like the dwarf with the two heads, who is so old that nobody can tell his age—you're a perpetual wonder—what is it that's done now, that seems to excite your alarm so?"

"Why, Granger has killed his wife at last," said Jones—who turned out himself to be a limb of the law—being constable, crier of the court, and subpœna-server on delinquent tax-payers.

"O, he has, has he?" said the district attorney—"let me have your tobacco, Jones."

Jones handed the legal representative of the state, or of that certain district of it, his honey-dew, and the D. A. having cut a chunk off it and deposited it in his jaw, coolly remarked—"You have summoned an inquest, and secured Granger, of course."

Jones.—"I have secured Granger, and an almighty tough job I had of it; but I reckon the body must be found first, 'fore there's an inquest. I don't know no law, if the Magistrate's Manual don't say, in an article on dead bodies, page 106, that there can't be no inquest where there aint no body found."

District Attorney—Contemptuously.—"O, Jones, I admit you're a most profound lawyer; but notice the judge; tell him I will be in court at ten o'clock—let him be there to hear this case; and I will be there to investigate it, in the name and on behalf of the sovereign state of Mississippi; but," descending from his dignity, "Jones, let us liquor before you go."

"Squire," said Jones, "you ought to be chancellor,

you ought. It's the first time I shook the dew off my boots this morning."

They liquored, and Jones went to obey the orders of him who had succeeded in ascending a few rounds above him on the legal ladder. Granger's murder of the wife of his bosom was the sole talk at the breakfast-table, and, indeed, of the whole village. No one exactly knew how the bloody and inhuman deed was perpetrated—nor where the body was: but all agreed that it was a most diabolical murder. They knew it would come to that, they said; they were always quarrelling, was Granger and his wife, and often drunk; it could not be otherwise. Blood was found on the floor, and on a knife that was found under the cupboard. But what could have been done with the body? One saw Granger sink a large box in the lake before day; another saw two young Saw-bones, from New Orleans, put off in a skiff a little after day, in which there was something in a sack; and a third noticed the earth freshly dug in the woods, at the rear of Granger's house.

Ten o'clock came, and the dingy log-cabin which formed the court-house was crowded. The judge sat on the bench, behind a huge pair of iron-cased spectacles; the district attorney was poring over a "dog-eared" edition of "Starkie on Evidence." Jones was sitting with his horseskin boots stuck upon the table before him and before the judge, his feet, of course, being in them; and Granger, the most unconcerned-looking man in court, was whittling a stick where he sat, to the right but in the rear of the bench.

"Are you prepared to proceed with this case, Mr. District Attorney?" said the judge.

"I am prepared, your honour," said the district attorney.

"Are *you* ready to proceed to preliminary trial, William Granger?" said the judge, with all the assumed solemn dignity of a marshal; "or, if you are not now, when will you?" he added.

"Just whenever you please," said Granger, in a maudlin tone of indifference; "but if Sal had taken my advice, this would never have happened. She ——"

"Silence, sir," said the judge; "in the first place you must learn to respect the court, and in the next place, you are not bound to tell any thing that will criminate yourself. Mr. District Attorney, proceed."

Granger muttered, "Criminate the d——l."

Jones called silence. The district attorney then took from between his teeth some masticated tobacco, and proceeded: "May it please this court, I am about to lay before you the skeleton—I say the skeleton—for the great body of facts are not yet fully developed. I am about to lay before you, I say, the skeleton of as foul a murder—as inhuman a murder—as unnatural a murder as was ever recorded in the annals of crime. [*Aside*—Jones, give me your tobaccer.] Yes, sir, a murder, which, considering the relations that existed between the murderer and his victim, would, as Shakspeare says, curl up a nigger's blood, and, what is harder still, make his hair stand on end, like the tail of a frightened gobbler! But, sir, although the manner in which this foul deed was perpetrated is at present shrouded in mystery—of the fact of the murder there is no doubt; the prisoner and his wife were heard quarrelling last evening; she has not been since seen. The traces of blood are visible on the floor, and a knife with clotted gore on it was discovered under the cupboard!"

Granger attempted to say something about the blood on the floor and on the knife being that of a chicken Sall killed the previous evening, but Jones called silence! and would permit him to make no explanation. The district attorney proceeded :—"I was saying, your honour, that up to this time, the body of the murdered wife has not been discovered. But, as 'murder speaks with most miraculous organ,' it will, no doubt, soon be seen."

And so, in truth, it was, for the district attorney had not well finished his quotation, when Mrs. Granger, all alive, protruding her head into the court, called out—"Consarn you, Bill Granger, is it there you be, instead of hoein' the taters! but when I was goin' to that ere quiltin' frolic of Mrs. Sharp's last evenin', I said you wouldn't do nothin' till I came back, and I knew you wouldn't—consarn your picter!"

It is unnecessary to say, that the appearance of Mrs. Granger, in proper person—in substance, not in shade—in court created no little consternation. The fear, which what was believed her apparition first occasioned, was succeeded on the part of the crowd by a unanimous burst of humour, but, on the part of the judge and the district attorney, by a consciousness that they had made themselves rather ridiculous. "I think we have proceeded far enough in this case," said the judge.

"I call for a conviction," said Jones. "I ain't a goin

to be chizzelled out of my fees for making the arrest, that way."

"Why the woman that you charged Granger with killing—his wife—stands before you!" said the judge, surprised at the absurdity of Jones's request.

"O, you can't come it, judge," said Jones. "I suppose you don't think I never read law; just hold on a while"—and he snatched up "Phillips on Evidence," turning to page 64, triumphantly read:—

"*As a party on record is not a competent witness—neither is the husband or wife of the party competent to give evidence either for or against the party*;" and throwing down the book, he exclaimed—"there, I believe that settles the pint; I believe, 'cording to law, Mrs. Granger ain't a competent witness to prove in favour of her husband in this case. I reckon not."

The court was dismissed. Granger and his wife went home, arguing, as usual, by the way; the spectators were convulsed with laughter at the termination of the awful murder case; the judge and the district attorney attributed the mistakes of the morning to that "fool, Jones," and Jones swore he would never make another arrest as long as he'd live.

KICKING A YANKEE.

BY JOS. M. FIELD, ESQ., OF THE ST. LOUIS "REVEILLE."

Few men of his age have written so much and so well as Mr. Field, whose contributions to the press, under the signatures of "Straws," "Everpoint," etc., etc., would make a large and most amusing series of pen and ink sketches. His facility of composition is not less surprising than his industry, for he has been for years either engaged in the laborious profession of the stage, or writing for a daily newspaper.

A VERY handsome friend of ours, who a few weeks ago was *poked* out of a comfortable office up the river, has betaken himself to Bangor, for a time, to recover from the wound inflicted upon his feelings by our "unprincipled and immolating administration."

Change of air must have had an instantaneous effect upon his spirits, for, from Galena, he writes us an amusing letter, which, among other things, tells us of a desperate quarrel that took place on board of the boat between a real live dandy tourist, and a real live Yankee settler. The latter trod on the toes of the former; whereupon the former threatened to "Kick out of the cabin" the latter.

"You'll kick me out of this cabing?"

"Yes, sir, I'll kick you out of this cabin!"

"You'll kick *me*, Mr. *Hitchcock*, out of this cabing?"

"Yes, sir, I'll kick *you*, Mr. Hitchcock!"

"Wal, I guess," said the Yankee, very coolly, after being perfectly satisfied that it was himself who stood in such imminent peril of assault—"I guess, since you talk of kicking, you've never heard me tell about old Bradley and my mare, there, to hum?"

"No, sir, nor do I wish——"

"Wal, guess it won't set you back much, any how, as kicking's generally best to be considered on. You see old Bradley is one of these sanctimonious, long-faced hypocrites, who put on a religious suit every Sabbath morning, and with a good deal of screwing, manage to keep it on till after sermon in the afternoon; and as I was a Universalist, he allers picked me out as a subject for religious conversation—and the darned hypocrite would talk about heaven, hell, and the devil—the crucifixion and prayer, without ever winking. Wal, he had an old roan mare that would jump over any fourteen-rail fence in Illinois, and open any door in my barn that hadn't a padlock on it. Tu or three times I found her in my stable, and I told Bradley about it, and he was 'very sorry'—'an unruly animal'—'would watch her,' and a hull lot of such things, all said in a very serious manner, with a face twice as long as old Deacon Farrar's on Sacrament day. I knew all the time he was lying, and so I watched him and his old roan tu; and for three nights regular, old roan came to my stable about bedtime, and just at daylight Bradley would come, bridle her, and ride off. I then just took my old mare down to a blacksmith's shop, and had some shoes made with 'corks' about four inches long, and had 'em nailed on to her hind feet. Your heels, mister, aint nuthing tu 'em. I took her home, give her about ten feet

"The Yankee had not ceased to advance, nor the dandy, in his astonishment to retreat."—*Page* 164.

halter, and tied her right in the centre of the stable, fed her well with oats about nine o'clock, and after taking a good smoke, went to bed, knowing that my old mare was a truth-telling animal, and that she'd give a good report of herself in the morning. I hadn't got fairly to sleep before the old 'oman hunched me and wanted to know what on airth was the matter out at the stable. Says I, 'Go tu sleep, Peggy, it is nothing but Kate—she is kicking off flies, I guess!' Purty soon she hunched me agin, and says she, 'Mr. Hitchcock, du git up and see what in the world is the matter with Kate, for she is kicking most powerfully.' 'Lay still, Peggy, Kate will take care of herself, I guess.' Wal, the next morning, about daylight, Bradley, with bridle in hand, cum to the stable, as true as the book of Genesis; when he saw the old roan's sides, starn, and head, he cursed and swore worse than you did, mister, when I came down on your toes. Arter breakfast that morning Joe Davis cum to my house, and says he, 'Bradley's old roan is nearly dead—she's cut all to pieces and can scarcely move.' 'I want to know,' says I, 'how on airth did it happen?' Now Joe Davis was a member of the same church with Bradley, and whilst we were talking, up cum that everlastin' hypocrite, and says he, 'Mr. Hitchcock, my old roan is ruined!' 'Du tell,' says I. 'She is cut all to pieces,' says he; 'do you know whether she was in your stable, Mr. Hitchcock, last night?' Wal, mister, with this I let out: 'Do I *know* it?'—(the Yankee here, in illustration, made a sudden advance upon the dandy, who made way for him unconsciously, as it were)—'Do I know it, you no-souled, shad-bellied, squash-headed, old night-owl you!—you hay-hookin', corn-cribbin', fodder-fudgin', cent-shavin', whitlin'-of-nuthin' you!—Kate kicks like a mere dumb beast, but I've reduced the thing to a *science!*'" The Yankee had not ceased to advance, or the dandy, in his astonishment, to retreat; and now, the motion of the latter being accelerated by an apparent demonstration on the part of the former to "suit the action to the word," he found himself in the "social hall," tumbling backwards over a pile of baggage, and tearing the knees of his pants as he scrambled up, a perfect scream of laughter stunning him from all sides. The defeat was total:—a few moments afterwards he was seen dragging his own trunk ashore, while Mr. *Hitch*cock finished his story on the boiler deck.

A "DOWN EAST" ORIGINAL.

BY "DE NOGBY," OF BOSTON.

"De Nogby" is an illustrious member of the renowned "Digby Club" of the "Modern Athens," as also of that time-honoured sodality, the "Mammoth Cod Association," which last recently celebrated its 267th anniversary! Since our promotion to the responsible situation of chairman of the "Committee on *Bimbo*," it is understood that "De Nogby" is prosecuting his studies at the Swimming School with the utmost assiduity, in the hope of an appointment to the "Committee on Drowning."

I WAS rash enough on the first of the month to go into the country to live, seduced by Ralph Waldo Emerson's laudation of Spring, and am heartily sick of it, for the wind has been on a blow ever since, and, like a big baby, made a child's rattle of every thing it could lay its hands to, from a "huckleberry" bush up to an orthodox meeting-house. But there is one consolation: my hen's nest is so arranged that the eggs fall directly from the fowl into my skillet of hot water; consequently I eat them fresher, perhaps, than they do at some boarding-houses, where the landladies appear to believe that they are not fit to cook until they have attained the *haut gout*. Or, perhaps, they keep them until they are *cheap* enough to eat, on the same principle that "Johnny L——" (of whom so many queer stories are told) kept his fish. "Johnny" was seen carrying home a piece of fresh salmon at a time when it was a dollar a pound; he was asked why he didn't wait until it was cheaper? "Aha!" replied Johnny, "I know what *I'm* about. I shall put it in my ice-chest, and when it gets down to twenty-five cents a pound, I shall eat it!"

Johnny is the same "stick" who set a light that the rats might see to go into his trap, and when asked by the painter what letter he would have put on the panel of his carriage, preferred W, because he thought it the best looking in the whole alphabet. He once marked up the prices of his goods in a dull season, and when he had finished the job went home and told his wife he had made a thousand dollars by the operation—forgetting that the merchandise yet remained to be sold. Told, once, that his store was on fire, he said it couldn't be, for he had the key in his pocket; and he is said to have ordered a huge thermometer to regulate the weather, and locked his door to keep the heat out. When he had killed his pig, he sagely remarked that "it didn't weigh as much as he expected, and he never thought it would." He sold half of his porker to a neighbour, but it was a question how it should be divided, after cutting it across in the middle. The neighbour proposed that L—— should put his hand unseen by him on one extremity or the other, and he'd say, without knowing what it was, whether he would have it or not. Johnny consented, and slightly cutting off the pig's curly termination, when his friend's back was turned, stuck it on the nose, and demanded, "Who shall have the part with the tail on?" "I!" exclaimed the other triumphantly. "Then you have got the fore-quarters!" said Johnny. On another occasion, some waggish butchers in the market persuaded him that it would improve the looks of his favourite dog to cut his tail shorter. Johnny assented, but fearing to trust the operation to any of the wags, he got them to hold the animal while he acted as surgeon, for he said he wanted only a very little amputated "to begin with." After calculating very nicely where to strike, Johnny raised the cleaver; at the same moment the butchers shoved the dog along, so that when the knife had fallen, the poor man found that he had severed his cur in twain, whereupon he protested, in perfect dismay, that "it was a little too short, by a d—d sight!"

"SOMEBODY IN MY BED!"

BY W. J. JONES, ESQ., OF HARRISBURG, PA.

We are not quite sure we have given Mr. J's. address correctly, but never mind, he *may* be a relative of that Hamilton C. Jones, Esq., of North Carolina, whose story of "Cousin Sally Dilliard" has for the twentieth time gone the rounds of the press. At any rate he sent the sketch below to the "Spirit of the Times" from Harrisburg, with a promise to become an occasional contributor—a promise which he has incontinently forgotten, to the great regret and mortification of the editor thereof and some tens of thousands of its readers.

A WEEK or two ago, during my peregrinations through northern Pennsylvania, spreading knowledge among the denizens thereof, (I sell books!) I "just dropt in" at a comfortable-looking inn, where I concluded to remain for a day or two. After a good substantial supper, I lit a "York County Principe," (the like of which sell in these regions at the rate of *four* for a penny,) and seated myself in the ring formed around the bar-room stove. There was the brawny butcher, the effeminate tailor, a Yankee fidler, two horse dealers, a speculator, a blackleg, the village Esculapius, and "the Captain," who, in consequence of being able to live on his means, was a person of no small importance, and therefore allowed to sit before the fire-stove with the poker to stir the fire—a mark of respect granted *only* to persons of standing.

Yarn after yarn had been spun and the hour for retiring had arrived—the landlord was dosing behind his bar,—and the spirit of the conversation was beginning to flag, when the doctor whispered to me that if I would pay attention, he would "top off" with a good one.

"I believe, captain," said the doctor, "I never told you about my adventure with a woman at my boarding house, when I was attending the lecture."

"No, let's have it," replied the individual addressed, who was a short, flabby, fat man of about fifty, with a highly nervous temperament, and a very red face.

"At the time I attended the lectures, I boarded at a house in which there were no females, but the landlady and an old coloured cook——"

(Here the doctor made a slight pause, and the captain, by way of requesting him to go on, said "Well.")

"I often felt the want of female society to soften the severe labours of deep study, and dispel the *ennui* to which I was subject——"

"Well," said the captain.

"But as I feared that forming acquaintances among the ladies might interfere with my studies, I avoided them all——"

"Well."

"One evening after listening to a long lecture on physical anatomy, and after dissecting a large negro, fatigued in body and mind, I went to my lodgings——"

"Well," said the captain.

"I went into the hall, took a large lamp, and went directly to my room, it being then after one o'clock——"

"Well!"

"I placed the light upon the table, and commenced

undressing. I had hardly got my coat off when my attention was attracted to a frock, and a quantity of petticoats lying on a chair near the bed——"

"Well!" said the captain, who began to show signs that he was getting deeply interested.

"And a pair of beautiful small shoes and stockings on the floor. Of course I thought it strange, and was about to retire—but then I thought as it was *my* room, I had at least a right to know who was in my bed——"

"Exactly," nodded the captain, "well!"

"So I took the light, went softly to the bed, and with a trembling hand drew aside the curtain. Heavens! what a sight! A young girl—I should say an angel, of about eighteen, was in there asleep——"

"Well!" said the captain, giving his chair a hitch.

"As I gazed upon her, I thought that I had never witnessed any thing more beautiful. From underneath a little night-cap, rivalling the snow in whiteness, fell a stray ringlet over a neck and shoulders of alabaster——"

"Well!" said the excited captain, giving his chair another hitch.

"Never did I look upon a bust more perfectly formed. I took hold of the coverlid and softly pulled it down——"

"Well!" said the captain, betraying the utmost excitement.

"To her waist——"

"*Well!!*" said the captain, dropping the paper, and renewing the position of his legs.

"She had on a night dress, buttoned up before, but softly I opened the two first buttons——"

"WELL!!!" said the captain, wrought to the highest pitch of excitement.

"And then, ye gods! what a sight to gaze upon—a Hebe—pshaw! words fail. Just then——"

"WELL!!!!" said the captain, hitching his chair right and left, and squirting his tobacco juice against the stove that it fairly fizzed again.

"I thought that I was taking a mean advantage of her, so I covered her up, seized my coat and boots, and went and slept in another room!"

"*It's a lie!*" shouted the excited captain, jumping up and kicking over his chair. "IT'S A LIE!"

A DAY AT SOL. SLICE'S.

BY "NAT. SLOCUM," OF SOUTH CAROLINA.

We would "give all our old clothes" and a new suit to boot, to shake hands with the writer of the sketch subjoined. Who he is, we doubt if "the oldest inhabitant" of Carolina can tell; certainly we have forgotten if we ever knew, but if we ever should be fortunate enough to meet him, if he does not "touch knees with us under mahogany" it shall not be our fault.

SHORTLY after my election, in 183–, I attended a review held at "Slice's Muster Ground." Before mounting my charger, I observed, tacked to a tree near me, a sheet of foolscap paper, on which was written, in letters of nearly an inch, the following:—

Dinner kin be had On the FoLLowin Tums at my HousE to Day priv8s thirty seven cents non comeishund ophisers 25 comeishund frEE i want you awl to ete dancin to beGin at won erclock awl them what dont wish to kevort will finD cards on the shelf in the cubberd ☞ licker On the uzual Tums

SOLOMON SLICE.

I had, by hard study, deciphered this fancy piece of handicraft, when old Slice came up.

"Aha, kunnel, I see the 'lection haint spiled you; you cares more for yer belly than you does for them muster fellows yit."

I assured him I did.

"Well, could you make it out? Some of them un-larnt fellers, Joe Smith, Tim Daly, and Bill Lever, the ugly son of a gun, 'lowed they didn't know what it was! Tim sed he reckined the old gobler must 'ave trod in the ink! Now, I don't see nothin' agin them letters. To be sure, that D is sot a *leetle* too forred; but the balance is as good as anybody kin do. I writ it big, so, as Scriptur' says, them what runs kin read."

"But why, Slice, do you make such difference in your charges?"

"Well, see here, kunnel, it don't much matter to me ef them privates don't come; but it is some credit to have fellers with eppletts on a settin' up to my vittles, and ef I do make a leetle sommat at the licker busness, it's you officers what has the muster here—so I gives you free seats."

I determined to be one of his guests that day, as I had heard he entertained well. So after parade I made my way back to Slice's, and found I was not a moment too early: dinner was already on a table spread in the yard. As I came up, old Sol. mounted the table, and cried out—at the same time waving a dirty dishcloth above his head—"Oh yis, gentle*men!* Oh yis! din ner's reddy! Come, awl of yer."

Fortune gave me a seat near Bill Lever, than whom it would be impossible to imagine a worse-looking or better-natured fellow. To attempt a description of him would be to make a failure. His face can bid defiance to the brush and palette of the best artist. On my right sat Tim Daly, "his shadder." Then began the clatter of knives and forks, interspersed with loud orders for "vittles." "More bread, here!" "Sol., you skunk, bring that mutton here!" "Beef, *beef*, BEEF!" from a burly old fellow, who was leaning back in his chair, his eyes shut tight, and mouth like a young mocking-bird. "Pass them taturs down this way, Uncle Slice—*that's* you;" and squealed out a little sallow-faced sandlapper —"More *cow*cumbers at this place!"

Old Sol. Slice was *raised* now. "You infernal copper-coloured sneak! jist get rite up from that table! You set there and holler as ef you *paid* fur yer dinner, 'stead of some pusson giving it to you! Jist hist, and take yourself off to that clay bank down thar! You wont be so much outen yer element *thar*, I reckin! Will you go, —— you?"

Cowcumber sloped.

"Is them your tums, Slice?" inquired Daly; "I thought the turkey writ out—I want you *awl* to ete."

"D—n you and the gobler too—I want awl to ete, but derned ef he's to ete *awl!* He's ete three plates of *cow*cumbers a'reddy."

"Uncle Sol.," now put in Lever, "don't you see yer bill is wrong? Now take my advice and have it altered by next mustering day; and I reckon you had better begin it this evenin', for you know it's a mity teedjus job."

"You ugly son of a gun!" muttered old Sol., going off—"yer mother ought to 'ave been ashamed of herself to 'ave *had* you; but, poor creetur, I reckin she couldn't help it."

"Mr. Lever," I asked, "why do these people always speak of you as 'ugly Bill Lever?' You do not think yourself bad-looking, do you?"

"Well, kunnel, I used to blieve I was only toloble good-looking, and remained in that blissful ignunce twell I was proved to be the ugliest man in all Charleston: and sence that, ef thar are anything that I humps myself on, it's my ugly."

"Proven to be the worst-looking man—how was that? Tell me."

"I never said wost-lookin—I sed *ugliest*—wost-lookin, the devil! Well, I went to Charleston, with brother Lije Lever—he's one of yer *wost-lookin* fellers—I'm ugly. As I was sayin', I went to town with him; we tuck a load of poultry—we made a right nice spec that trip, too. Well, arter we had laid in some shugar, and coffee, and some necessaries, we was——"

"Stop!" interrupted Daly. "What do you mean by necessaries?"

"Licker."

"I thought so—go on."

"Well, arter gitting them things, we started for home. As we was comin' up King Street——"

"Stop!" again interrupted Daly. "Who was drivin'?"

"Brother Lije."

"Aha, and you was in the wagin on top the bar'l, as uzual."

"I was in the waggin. Ef you don't hush, Tim, I'll quit. We had got a matter of about half-way up the street, when a dandy, dressed in the hite of fashun, and mounted on a blood bay hoss, came canterin' down ahead of us. All at wunst he drawed up by the side of Lije, and ses he, 'I've found him at last.'

"'Found *what?*' sez Lije.

"'Why,' sez the dandy, 'I'll bet you ten dollars you are the ugliest man in Charleston.'

"Sez Lije, very coolly, sez he, 'I never bets, mister; but I'm not deservin' of that honour; I'll show you what is;' and turning in his saddle to'ards me, 'Poke yer head out, Billy,' sez he. No sooner said than done: I histed the waggin-sheet, and looked out on him. I never did see a feller so sot back! There he stood a gazin' at me—I thought he was demented. At last, comin' too a little, he sez to me, 'You need not git out, my friend—your *face* is sufficient to convince me. And, though you didn't bet,' sez he, turnin' to Lije, 'I think you fully deserve the ten. Here it is. I thank you, gentlemen, for the finest site that ever my eyes feasted upon. Good mornin';' and he rode off."

Here Lever ceased speaking, and fell to eating very rapidly, as if he wished to make up for lost time.

"Why don't you go on, Bill, and tell the kunnel about the balance of that trip?" inquired Tim Daly.

"'Cause you kin do it as well as me, and I've got to the innard man now."

"Kunnel, Bill don't like to tell this, for ef thar are

anything he humps hisself on *besides ugly*, it is his manners among the fimmales, and I'll say it here before him; he does please the gals fust rate. A grate beau is Bill. The day he left Charleston he dipped inter that gin bar'l putty freekwent, in konsequence of which he was, as one might say, travellin' incogniter all that evening.

"Well, next morning he wanted warter the worst sort; so the fust house he comes to, he goes up to the gate, and hollered, 'Keeps house?' A tall man come out and wanted to know his will. Then it was he stared. Did you ever see a greenhorn at a animal show? Ef you has, then you kin have *some* idear of the look he give Bill.

"'Could a body git some warter, ef you please?'

"The man stared afresh—so Bill began opening the gate.

"'Stop, for heaven's sake,' sez the man; 'I'll have it brought to you.—Don't come in—my wife is in a very delicut way, and the frite might cause a flustration.'"

"That's a durned lie," shouted Lever. "Come, boys, let's go in among the gals—I hear the fiddle."

We then adjourned to the "ball-room," which we found crowded with dancers already on the floor.

"Come, kunnel," said Slice, "here is Miss Patsey Jaggers, jest from town, and the best dancer in the room: let me interduce you."

Sol. took my arm—led me across the room—and, in all due form, presented me. I made my congee, and solicited the "exquisite pleasure, the ecstatic delight,"

&c., which she readily promised. We conversed about "town" and the people with whom she had there become acquainted. I found her much more intelligent than the girls one generally meets at such places.

"Take dem pardners, gemplemen," sung out Long Ben, an old negro, who had *fiddled* for that "beat" for the last quarter of a century. I immediately led out Miss Patsey Jaggers, intending to take the "head."

"Col. Slokum," said she, "I see it is well for you I came to-day; I know these people well. They do not like strangers to take, what they call, *liberties*—it would be better, therefore, that we should be second, rather than first, in this reel; and you need not be very precise in your steps; but if you know any *negro* dances, fire away at them!"

When a boy, the negroes, at their frolics on my father's plantation, had initiated me into all the "sleights" of which their African legs were capable; and on this day they stood me a good turn. When my time came, therefore, I took "a hop, skip, and a jump" towards my partner, "racked back on my hind feet a little," then commenced "the double shuffle," "pigeon-wing on the floor," "de same in de ar," "Pete Jonson's knock," "the under cleets," and other *refined* steps, "too numerous to mention;" and finally finished off on "old trimble toes"—a rare and difficult movement.—I saw that I had succeeded, for shouts of applause for "the kunnel" came from all quarters of the room. "Go it, kunnel; you're a trump!" "Look at him, Jake! what do you think of that?" "Why, the man hain't a bone in him!" "He stands back on his hind feet like a venison." "I wish I had him in my barn; he'd tramp out wheat nice"—and such other comments caused me to hold high my haughty head.

"Bill, now it's yer time," said our beef man. "You are allers good, but I has a faint idear that you has here met yer ekal."

"Two to one on that," squealed out Cowcumber. "I knows Bill well, and I'll go you an independent on his beating yon feller bad."

Lever now began, with a smile on his ugly countenance, and—to my mortification—went through every movement of mine with *more* ease; and in "casting off" he even introduced a *new* step, which would be as difficult to describe as to perform. He called it the *windin blades.*

"Never care, Col.," said my partner; "after this reel, we will risk a waltz together: and my word for it, you will yet win."

The truth is, I did feel miserable, and was impatient to get through.—Immediately, therefore, after the others had taken their seats, I asked Long Ben to play a waltz. By a lucky chance he once had learned *one:* and, as he drew his bow, I started off with my partner. Round and around we went, to the astonishment of all, they never having witnessed any thing of the kind. Miss Patsey was a fine mover, and really one of the most graceful waltzers I have ever seen. As for myself, I was delighted with the ease and action I displayed on that occasion.

"Do not let it become too common," whispered my fair one. I conducted her to a chair, *now* perfectly satisfied with my success.

"Dem is de best dat ever happunt in dis beat," said Long Ben.

"Kunnel, you've won," said Lever, with a hang-dog expression of countenance; "but I'm one what never yit did give up in a dance, of any kind: so, if I kin git a gal, I'll try that lick."

After some persuasion he "got a gal," and, calling on old Ben to "scrape them cat entrails," made an attempt, but found they could not get off. It was something like two unbroken colts when first put in harness; they could not start together. At last Bill bellowed out—"Here's what never baulks," and began to turn, pulling her after him. About the third evolution of this kind, the gal's feet parted company with the floor, and lifted themselves upon a level with her head. I only saw a red petticoat, and—being a modest man—turned my back upon this "pair of revolvers." I could not, however, stop my ears from the remarks of the old woman.

"Oh, *my* Lord!" shrieked old Mrs. Spraggs, "that's *too* bad, to have a feller-creatur's legs a flyin' in that stile."

"Yes," was the observation of that spiteful old maid, Miss Jemima Clipps, "purticularly ef the feller-creetur's legs happun to be crooked. I would advise all you young gals to look at yer legs before you undertake anything you ain't used to. Crooked legs is mity bad in them turnin' dances."

I knew, from the noise behind me, that Bill was "keeping even along;" when suddenly the noise was increased a thousand-fold; and on old Mrs. Spraggs exclaiming "thar," I turned in time to see Lever stretched on the floor, and his gal just "settling upon him." Old Mrs. Spraggs,—kind-hearted old soul—ran to her assistance, and while picking her up *whispered*, as all old ladies do, so as to be heard by all—"Git up, Sall, all these fellers couldn't a seed more ef you was married to 'em all." The "gall" arose to her feet, dealing blows, right and left, upon poor Bill—"Take that, and that, for histin' me up before all these people, you onmannerly, ugly piece of deformity."

"I beg pardon, Sall," pleaded Lever, "I couldn't help it—I wouldn't a done it ef I had knowed! you knows I was on this eend of you and couldn't see nuthin'."

The Amazon became doubly enraged at this, and raising a chair, she threw it at Lever with such force, that, had it done its errand, would have given him his quietus. He adroitly avoided it, however, and escaped through the door. She seemed perfectly satisfied with this *manly* effort at redress; and in a short time looked as if nothing had happened to disturb her peace of mind.

Going into an adjoining room, I found Tim Daly playing "old Sledge" with Cowcumber—five cents a game. Fortune seemed to have favoured the sand-lapper, if one might judge from the number of pieces at his elbow. I stayed to watch the game. After a few deals the luck turned. Cowcumber lost two or three games, when, suddenly pressing both his hands upon his stomach, he emitted some of the most piteous groans that ever came from the breast of man.

"Aha, old feller, you want to come that same old game on me, do you?"

"Oh, but, Tim, do let me go, now, I'll be back *directly*. I tuckt some ile this mornin', and that *must* be attended to."

"No, I tell you, sir, ile or no ile, I don't kere what you do with yourself—thar you sets twell *I* say you kin git up; and I needn't be so purticular in my observations to you as to say, *that* won't be ontwell all that pile comes back inter my hands. You've tricked me before, and as I know yer derned herrin' belly don't trouble you when you are winnin', I'm determined it shan't pester you when yer loosing."

Tim made good his word; in half an hour he had won it all, and that without an accident.

Thus the day was passed, in dancing, drinking, card-playing, and fighting. One "engage*ment*" may be mentioned. It was not fought on that day, however, but spoken of by "our beef-man."

About twelve o'clock that night, he, together with two or three others, might have been seen seated on the staircase. Cowcumber was among their number. They seemed to have had a "war talk."

"Talking about fightin'," says Beef, "aminds me of a engage*ment* what tuck place atween Joe Humphries and Sam Higgins once. I ain't a goying to tell you 'nother quarrel—*that* would take too long a time: they was at it two years therseffs. Findally, howsomedever, they yoked at Spartinbug Court House. Now, you what hain't the *faintest* idear of what fightin' is, won't b'lieve what I'm bout to *no*rate. But, as I was a sayin', they yoked, and they fit, *and* they fit, and I *do* reckin, in all their backin's *and* forrerdin's they kivered nigh two acres of ground. *Hit* was floatin' in blood!

You might a githered a half a gallon of years, and thumbs, and fingers, and noses! They would bite pieces outen one another and spit 'em out agin, and take a fresh holt, and when they let *that* go the piece would be in ther mouth. They had been fitin' one solid hour, when I got sick and quit the field."

"Which whoopt," inquired Cowcumber.

"I don't know, I left 'em fightin'! the last I heared from thar they was fightin', and I do reckin ther at it yet—its a vinemous fite."

"Who is *he*," I asked of Lever.

"Why, that's Jack Wood*ruff*—he's the derndest, biggest, *onremittentest* liar from Charleston to the mountings!'

CUPPING ON THE STERNUM.

BY H. C. L., OF MISSISSIPPI.

A new-fledged disciple of Æsculapius is the writer of the following sketch, in which is displayed, in bold relief, one of "the ills which flesh is heir to," when subjected to the tender mercies of inexperienced medical practitioners. As H. C. L., like "The Razor-Strop-Man," has "a few more left, of the same sort," we trust when he reads this paragraph he will forthwith set to work and give us some more extracts from "The Diary of a Young Physician."

I HAD been a student of medicine about three weeks, and had got as far as cupping, cathartics, and castor oil, in the noble science of physic, when, as I was sitting in the office, investigating by induction the medicinal properties of a jar of tamarinds, I received a note from my preceptor which ran thus:—

"Mr. L.—You will please take the large cups and scarificator, together with a large blister, up to Mr. J.. and cup his negro girl Chaney very freely over the *sternum ;* after you have cupped her, apply the blister over the same, as she has inflammation of the lungs."

In anatomy, the *sternum* is that portion of the osseous system known in common parlance as the "breast bone," but at that time I was ignorant of the fact. I had not studied anatomy, and in my ignorance and simplicity of heart, imagined that the doctor wanted her to be cupped and blistered "a posteriori," or in other words, over the "seat," and that he had put the "um" to the "stern" in the note, merely for sport, or, it might have been the Latin termination of the word "stern." Filled with a sense of the delicacy and momentous import of my duty, I provided myself with the necessaries, and proceeded to cup Chaney on the *sternum.*

By way of parenthesis, let me create an idea of my patient, so that you may appreciate the field of my operation.

Just imagine a butcher's block five feet long and four feet through at the butt, converted into a fat bouncing negro wench, with smaller blocks appended for limbs, and you will have a faint conception of the figure and proportions of the delectable portion of humanity upon whom my curative capabilities were to be exhibited.

"How are you to-day, Chaney?" said I, as entering the cabin of my patient, I stood before her.

"Oh, massa young doctor," said she, "I does feel 'mazing bad—the mis'ry in my bosom almost broke my heart; I can scasely perspere," (*re*-spire, I suppose she meant, as, judging from the big drops which, like ebony beads, chased each other down her gleaming neck, I thought that she perspired beautifully.)

"I am very sorry to hear it, Chaney; the doctor has sent me up here to cup and blister you, and I hope it will relieve you entirely."

"Well, the Lord's will and the doctor's be done; this anguished sister be's ready"—and she proceeded to divest her bosom of its concealments, thinking that she had to be cupped over the seat of the pain; but it was a different *seat* than that, which my cups were destined to exhaust the atmosphere from.

"Stop, Chaney, I was not told to cup you on the breast, but on the *sternum*, so you'll have to turn over!"

"What!" shrieked she, rising straight up in the bed, a great deal whiter in the face than she had been for many a day; "you cup me on de *starn!* Massa young doctor, *tell* me, for de lub of prostituted 'manity, is you in airnest? Oh no, certainly, you is just joking—just making 'musement of de 'stresses of dis female!"

"No, Chaney, there is no mistake. The doctor says you must be cupped there, and it must and shall be done, so get ready."

"Oh, massa doctor, you must be mistaken—you must indeed! De pain no dere, but in my breast! How cupping dere goin' cure pain in de breast, eh? Tell me dat!"

"Well, Chaney, I don't know that I can do that, exactly, but I suppose it will be by sympathy. You know the stern and the bosom are not many feet apart. Any how, I am going to cup you there, if I have to call in help, so you had better consent."

Chaney, seeing that there was no retreat, agreed at last to the operation. Click! click! went the scarificator, and amidst the shouts of the patient and my awful solicitude for fear I might cut an artery, the "deed was did." But no blood flowed, nothing but grease, which trickled out slowly like molasses out of a worm hole. I saw that the cups were too in*fat*uated to draw blood from that quarter, so I removed them and applied the blister, and I expect fly-ointment was in demand about that time.

"Stop, Chaney, I was not told to cup you on the breast, but on the *sternum*, so you'll have to turn over!"—*Page* 186.

When the doctor returned, after an absence of several hours, he found the patient *entirely relieved*, and a blister drawn with about a tubful of water in its interior. I reckon she used chairs mighty little for a few weeks, and she hated the idea of the operation so bad that she burnt up a bran new dress just because it was *bum*bazine, and reminded her, by the first syllable, of the *seat* of "Cupping on the Sternum."

A BEAR STORY.

BY THE LATE WM. P. HAWES, ESQ., OF NEW YORK.

We have in a previous page alluded to the popularity of the author of the following story, as a humorous prose writer. Any article over the signature of "J. Cypress, jr.," was regarded with as much interest as that of "Boz." The following sketch gives a good idea of his peculiar style. We must premise that the scene of the story annexed was a fishing-hut on Fire Island, (a few miles from Long Island,) where a select sporting party were spending the night. The conversation which introduces Venus Raynor's story of the bear, refers to the "Shark Story," published in previous pages of this volume.

"WHAT an infernal lie!" growled Daniel.

"Have my doubts;" suggested the somnolent Peter Probasco, with all the solemnity of a man who knows his situation; at the same time shaking his head and spilling his liquor.

"Ha! ha! ha! Ha! ha! ha!" roared all the rest of the boys together.

"Is he done?" asked Raynor Rock.

"How many shirks was there?" cried long John, putting in his unusual lingual oar.

"That story puts me in mind," said Venus Raynor, "about what I've heerd tell on Ebenezer Smith, at the time he went down to the North Pole on a walen' voyage."

"Now look out for a screamer," laughed out Raynor Rock, refilling his pipe. "Stand by, Mr. Cypress, to let the sheet go."

"Is there any thing uncommon about that yarn, Venus?"

"Oncommon! well, I expect it's putty smart and oncommon for a man to go to sea with a bear, all alone, on a bare cake of ice. Captain Smith's woman used to say she couldn't bear to think on't."

"Tell us the whole of that, Venus," said Ned,—"that is, if it is true. Mine was—the whole of it,—although Peter has his doubts."

"I can't tell it as well as Zoph can; but I've no 'jections to tell it my way, no how. So, here goes—that's great brandy, Mr. Cypress." There was a gurgling sound of "something-to-take," running.

"Well, they was down into Baffin's Bay, or some other o' them cold Norwegen bays at the north, where the rain freezes as it comes down, and stands up in the air, on winter mornens, like great mountens o' ice, all in streaks. Well, the schooner was layen at anchor, and all the hands was out into the small boats, looken for wales,—all except the capting, who said he wa'n't very well that day. Well, he was walken up and down, on deck, smoken and thinking, I expect, mostly, when all of a sudden he reckoned he see one o' them big white bears—polar bears, you know—big as thunder—with long teeth. He reckoned he see one on 'em sclumpen along on a great cake o' ice, that lay on the leeward side of the bay, up agin the bank. The old capting wanted to kill one o' them varments most wonderful, but he never lucked to get a chance. Now tho', he thought, the time had come for him to walk into one on 'em at laast, and fix his mutton for him right. So he run forrad and lay hold onto a small skiff, that was layen near the forc'stal, and run her out and launched her. Then he tuk a drink, and—here's luck—and put in a stiff load of powder, a couple of balls, and jumped in, and pulled away for the ice.

"It wa'n't long 'fore he got 'cross the bay, for it was a narrer piece o' water—not more than haaf a mile wide—and then he got out on to the ice. It was a smart and large cake, and the bear was 'way down to the tother end on it, by the edge o' the water. So, he walked fust strut along, and then when he got putty cloast he walked 'round catecorned-like—likes's if he was drivin for a plain plover—so that the bear would'nt think he was comen arter him, and he dragged himself along on his hands and knees, low down, mostly. Well, the bear didn't seem to mind him none, and he got up within 'bout fifty yards on him, and then he looked so savage and big—the bear did—that the captain stopped and rested on his knees, and put up his gun, and he was agoin to shoot. But just then the bear turned round and snuffed up the captin—just as one of Lif's hounds snuffs up an old buck, Mr. Cypress,—and begun to walk towards him, slowly like. He come along, the captin said, clump, clump, very slow, and made the ice bend and crack again under him, so that the water come up and putty much kivered it all over. Well, there the captin was all the time squat on his knees, with his gun pinted, waiten for the varment to come up, and his knees and legs was mighty cold by means of the water that the bear riz on the ice as I was mentionen. At last the bear seemed to make up his mind to see how the captin *would* taste, and so he left off walkin slow, and started off on a smart and swift trot, right towards the old man, with his mouth wide open, roaren, and his tail sticken out stiff. The captain kept still, looken out all the time putty sharp, I should say, till the beast got within about ten yards on him, and then he let him have it. He aimed right at the fleshy part of his heart, but the bear dodged at the flash, and rared up, and the balls went into his two hind legs, just by the jynt, one into each, and broke the thigh bones smack off, so that he went right down aft, on the ice, thump, on his hind quarters, with nothen standen but his fore legs, and his head riz up, a growlen at the captin. When the old man see him down, and tryen to slide along the ice to get his revenge, likely, thinks he to himself, thinks he, I might as well get up and go and cut that ere creter's throat. So he tuk out his knife and opened it. But when he started to get up, he found, to his astonishment, that he was fruz fast to the ice. Don't laugh: it's a fact; there an't no doubt. The water, you see, had been round him a smart and long while, whilst he was waiten for the bear, and it's wonderful cold in them regions, as I was sayen, and you'll freeze in a minit if you don't keep moven about smartly. So the captin he strained first one leg, and then he strained tother, but he couldn't move 'em none. They was both fruz fast into the ice, about an inch and a half deep, from knee to toe, tight as a Jersey oyster perryauger on a mud flat at low water. So he laid down his gun, and looked at the bear, and doubled up his fists. 'Come on, you bloody varmint,' says the old man, as the bear swalloped along on his hinder eend, comen at him. He kept getten weaker, tho', and comen slower and slower all the time, so that at last, he didn't seem to move none; and directly, when he'd got so near that the captin could jist give him a dig in the nose by reachen forrard putty smart and far, the captin see that the beast was fruz fast too, nor he coudn't move a step further forrard no ways. Then the captin burst out a laughen, and clapped his hands down on to his thighs, and roared. The bear seemed to be most onmighty mad at the old man's fun, and set up such a growlen that what should come to pass, but the ice cracks and breaks all around the captin and the bear, down to the water's edge, and the wind jist then a shiften, and comen off shore, away they floated on a cake of ice about ten by six, off to sea, without the darned a biscot or a quart o' liquor to stand 'em on the cruise! There they sot, the bear and the captin, just so near that when they both reached forrads, they could jist about touch noses, and nother one not able to move any part on him, only excepten his upper part and fore paws."

"By jolly! that was rather a critical predicament, Venus," cried Ned, buttoning his coat. "I should have thought that the captain's nose and ears and hands would have been frozen too."

"That's quite naytr'l to suppose, sir, but you see the

bear kept him warm in the upper parts, by being so cloast to him, and breathen hard and hot on the old man whenever he growled at him. Them polar bears is wonderful hardy animals, and has a monstrous deal o' heat into 'em, by means of their bein able to stand such cold climates, I expect. And so the captin knowed this, and whenever he felt chilly, he just tuk his ramrod and stirred up the old rascal, and made him roar and squeal, and then the hot breath would come pouren out all over the captin, and made the air quite moderat and pleasant."

"Well, go on, Venus. Take another horn first."

"Well, there a'nt much more on't. Off they went to sea, and sometimes the wind druv 'em nothe, and then agin it druv 'em southe, but they went southe mostly; and so it went on until they were out about three weeks. So at last, one afternoon"——

"But, Venus, stop: tell us, in the name of wonder, how did the captain contrive to support life all this time?"

"Why, sir, to be sure, it was a hard kind o' life to support, but a hardy man will get used to almost"——

"No, no: what did he eat? what did he feed on?"

"O—O—I'd liked to've skipped that ere. Why, sir, I've heerd different accounts as to that. Uncle Obe Verity told me he reckoned the captin cut off one of the bear's paws, when he lay stretched out asleep, one day, with his jack-knife, and sucked that for fodder, and they say there's a smart deal o' nourishment in a white bear's foot. But if I may be allowed to spend my 'pinion, I should say my old man's account is the rightest, and that's—what's as follows. You see after they'd been out three days abouts, they begun to grow kind o' hungry, and then they got friendly, for misery loves company, you know; and the captin said the bear looked at him several times, very sorrowful, as much as to say, 'Captin, what the devil shall we do?' Well, one day they was sitten looken at each other, with the tears ready to burst out o' their eyes, when all of a hurry, somethin come floppen up out o' the water onto the ice. The captin looked and see it was a seal. The bear's eyes kindled up as he looked at it, and then, the captin said, he giv him a wink to keep still. So there they sot, still as starch, till the seal not thinken nothin o' them no more nor if they was dead, walked right up between 'em. Then slump! went down old whitey's nails into the fish's flesh, and the captin run his jack-knife into the tender loin. The seal soon got his bitters, and the captin cut a big hunk off the tail eend, and put it behind him, out o' the bear's reach, and then he felt smart and comfortable, for he had stores enough for a long cruise, though the bear couldn't say so much for himself.

"Well, the bear, by course, soon run out o' provisions, and had to put himself onto short allowance; and then he begun to show his natural temper. He first stretched himself out as far as he could go, and tried to hook the captin's piece o' seal, but when he found he couldn't reach that, he begun to blow and yell. Then he'd rare up and roar, and try to get himself clear from the ice. But mostly he rared up and roared, and pounded his big paws and head upon the ice, till by-an'-by (jist as the captin said he expected) the ice cracked in two agin, and split right through between the bear and the captin and there they was on two different pieces o' ice, the captin and the bear! The old man said he raaly felt sorry at parten company, and when the cake split and separate, he cut off about a haaf o' pound o' seal and chucked it to the bear. But either because it wan't enough for him, or else on account o' his feelen bad at the captin's goen, the beast wouldn't touch it to eat it, and he laid it down, and growled and moaned over it quite pitiful. Well, off they went, one one way, and t'other 'nother way, both feel'n pretty bad, I expect. After a while the captin got smart and cold, and felt mighty lonesome, and he said he raaly thought he'd a gi'n in and died, if they hadn't pick'd him up that arternoon."

"Who picked him up, Venus?"

"Who? a codfish craft off o' Newfoundland, I expect. They didn't know what to make o' him when they first see him slingen up his hat for 'em. But they got out all their boats, and took a small swivel and a couple o' muskets aboard, and started off—expecten it was the sea-sarpent, or an old maremaid. They woudn't believe it was a man, until he'd told 'em all about it, and then they didn't hardly believe it nuther; and they cut him out o' the ice and tuk him aboard their vessel, and rubbed his legs with ile o' vitrol; but it was a long time afore they come to."

"Didn't they hurt him badly in cutting him out, Venus?"

"No, sir, I believe not; not so bad as one migh

s'pose: for you see he'd been stuck in so long, that the circulaten on his blood had kind o' rotted the ice that was right next to him, and when they begun to cut, it crack'd off putty smart and easy, and he come out whole like a hard biled egg."

"What became of the bear?"

"Can't say as to that, what became o' him. He went off to sea somewheres, I expect. I should like to know, myself, how the varment got along right well, for it was kind in him to let the captin have the biggest haaf o' the seal, any how. That's all, boys. How many's asleep?"

PLAYING "POKER" IN ARKANSAS,

In which is shown, that if walls have ears, they may have voices.

BY A RESIDENT OF THAT "NECK OF TIMBER."

The Arkansas "Intelligencer," published at Van Buren, is not only extremely well edited, but it numbers among its correspondents some of the cleverest men west of the Mississippi. The gentlemen alluded to are occasional contributors to the "Spirit of the Times," which boasts of "a baker's dozen" of them, including "N. of Arkansas," an Ex-Governor, Albert Pike, the famous "Col. Pete Whitstone of the Devil's Fork of the Little Red," and other celebrities in the literary and sporting world.

Any one who may have had the good fortune to have laid eyes on the "Chart of this Neck of Timber," drawn from actual surveys, and presented, in conformity with a resolution of the Kraked Klub of Fort Gibson, to "Old Festivity, president of the Mystic Club of Van Buren,"—we say good fortune to have laid eyes on one of those charts, for there is very few in existence, and those zealously preserved by the lucky possessors thereof, must have noticed the locality of the "Prairie Store," situated on a commanding eminence about one mile east of south from the fort. To that spot we wish to direct the attention of the reader.

The "Prairie Store," owned by Mr. ——, has been long occupied by the owner as a mercantile establish ment. The building itself is of considerable dimensions, built of logs neatly put together, pointed and white-washed, whilst a number of scattered out-houses, such as kitchens, barns, stables, and the like, lend to the *tout ensemble* quite a village-like appearance. Among the several out-houses connected with and situated directly in the rear of the "Store," is one used formerly and for a length of time as a bakery. This one had been rented and recently fitted up as a gambling-house, by an individual of sporting or rather gambling notoriety, generally known throughout the county under the soubriquet of *Cherokee Brown*.

The building was composed of two rooms, one in which Mr. B's. *tricks* were most imposingly spread upon a stationary table at one end, with barely a sufficiency of space between it and the wall, for that gentleman to sit whilst in the pursuit of his profession. The room was lined with clap boards, of which material the entire building was composed, with a low incapacious loft overhead, which was the locale of his sleeping apartment, the entrance to which lay through a square hole in the ceiling of the adjoining room.

For the purpose intended, this spot was most admirably chosen; for situated as it is, very nearly in the centre of the neighbourhood, and surrounded as it was, at inconsiderable distances, with quite a number of *Board Taverns* and *Groceries*, the "Prairie Store" has become the rendezvous of the denizens and sojourners of this "Nick of Timber."

We are quite partial to the antique, and have ever held in high veneration the quaint old maxims which have been handed down to us since the "good old days of Adam and Eve," and there is one among those wise old sayings which reads, if we do not greatly mistake, "Give the devil his due," the charity of which we are in nowise inclined to contest or oppose ; and are, therefore, quite willing to admit that much credit is most certainly due the dashy projector of the scheme, for the tact he displayed both in the choice of locality and the various tricks devised to avoid the prolixity of a well-contested game, to enhance the chances in his favour, and to transfer with more ease and rapidity any moneys from the pockets of his *customers* to those of his own. Among other tricks devised by the gentleman of the sombre appellation, that of the *trumpet* deserves to be recorded.

The mechanism of the trumpet was such as at once to announce in its originator no inconsiderable knowledge of the philosophy of sounds. From the loft over the gambling-room, and leading along the floor, and downwards between the weather-boarding and ceiling, to a point about four feet from the ground, and directly in rear of the chair usually occupied by B., a tube of an inch diameter was arranged. Several small holes in the ceiling gave to a person above the opportunity of perceiving, at a glance, the contents of the hands of those whose backs were towards him, whilst the lowest whisper through the tube was conducted with the utmost distinctness to the ear of him who occupied the chair, and yet could not be heard one foot beyond. Of course B. required an accomplice for the successful prosecution of the game, and with a most efficient one was he provided, who will be introduced to the reader in his proper place. Such was the mechanism of the trumpet, the star invention of the age. Every thing had been most artfully prepared, and a game was only wanting to prove its efficiency. Happily they had not long to await, but were soon accommodated, and in the end received more than they had bargained for.

On a certain evening towards the close of last September, a large crowd of sporting characters, as was usual, had gathered at the "store," among whom was a sturdy native of the mountain districts of the "Old North State," over six feet in perpendicular measurement, and of uncommon bone and sinew; he looked any thing but his name, which by that singular license of nomenclature that indiscriminately gives dark names to fair people, and mechanical ones to any thing but artizans, had allotted him the *buoyant* name of Cork. *Faro* had been the order of the day, but on the approach of night, *Brown* had bantered the hardy mountaineer, who was said to be a brag player, for a game of poker, which was instantly taken up.

After the usual supper hour, the two retired to the gambling room, and locking themselves in, were soon deep into the mysteries by pairs and flushes. The game terminated at a late hour, considerably in favour of Cork. The next day the game was continued, but now, contrary to all precedents, luck was a dead letter, and science yielded to art. Cork was beat from the commencement. The strongest cards which fell to his hand yielded but the bare *ante*, whilst no brag of his remained uncoiled when his opponent was superior. Suspecting some trick was being played upon him, he racked his brains to discover the secret. The cards were minutely examined, and every motion of his antagonist narrowly scrutinized, but in vain; till at length making a large brag on no pair, he observed Brown lean back in his chair, his head resting against the wall as though he was deliberating within himself the policy of calling and the probability of winning. At that moment a vague and indescribable thought flashed across his mind.

"Fifty dollars better, you say?" observed Brown.

"There's the money, you can see for yourself."

"Well," said Brown, hesitatingly, "I call."

"No pair," said Cork.

"No pair," returned Brown.

"You beat me, I know."

"I've nothing but a single king," observed Brown.

"That beats me, but by G—d I'll find out this trick, or die in my tracks!" vociferated Cork, at the same time drawing forth his bowie-knife and rising from his chair.

Satisfied within himself that he had been tricked, his suspicions were directed over head. The first room was narrowly searched, and then the adjoining one, and then his attention was immediately directed to the square aperture in the loft, which was at the time closed with hay, as though that portion of the building was filled with the particular commodity. Unhesitatingly he mounted, easily removing the little hay that lay over the hole, which was indeed only used as a blind, and ascended to the loft. Profound darkness reigned there above, and while groping his way to the opposite end of the house, he stumbled against the body of some person, who, like a sleeping man when disturbed, turned over on his back, and went, accordingly, through all the preliminary steps of returning consciousness.

"Who in the h—l are you, and what are you doing here?"

"Why, it's me, Rothrock, I was up till day-break, and stole up here to take a nap," groaned that individual, who is too well known throughout all this neck of woods to make a description of him at all needful.

"But what's the matter with you, Cork?"

"I've been tricked, and I am right after unravelling it!"

By degrees, his eyes becoming accustomed to the darkness, he perceived the tin tube which lay along the floor, leading to the wall, and downwards. To tear it from the floor, and trace it to its termination was the work of but a few seconds. During this time, however, Brown having an eye to his own individual merit and corporeal safety, had decamped with his money and his *faro tools*, and deposited them at the "store." Soon after, Cork sallied from the house, bearing in his arms several yards of tin pipe, which he amused himself chopping up, to the great edification of the crowd. Rothrock, too, emerged from his *den*, and arming himself with something similar to a blunderbuss, had retired to a room adjoining the store. Cork having made a finish of the pipe, and his rage still unabated, looked around him for something else whereon to vent his fury. Recollecting Rothrock, and satisfied he was B.'s accomplice, he broke of in pursuit, and discovering that individual, he seized him by the throat and dashed him to the earth, and notwithstanding the coward's reiterated prayers for mercy, kicked and cuffed him to his heart's content.

Brown reappeared in the scene armed *cap-à-pie*, and

murder *might* have ensued had not some person interposed, and proposed that each party should abide the decision of three umpires. The proposition was acceded to, and three individuals selected, who, upon consultation, decided that the affair should terminate in Brown's refunding to Cork an amount sufficient to place him as he stood at the beginning of the game.

Brown, being glad to get off without bones being broken, came to the conclusion that it would be wise to emigrate, and went off at strides of about nine and a half feet to the lay down and picked it up like rats fighting, and has not been heard of since.

THE END.

www.ingramcontent.com/pod-product-compliance
Lightning Source LLC
LaVergne TN
LVHW011208110826
845150LV00006B/1369

* 9 7 8 1 4 2 5 5 1 8 1 2 7 *